DEATH IS NO STRANGER

A Jungle Missionary Series Novel – Book 2

by

ERNIE BOWMAN

FOOL'S PRESS
Ypsilanti, Michigan

Copyright 2021 by
Ernie Bowman
Fool's Press

All rights reserved. No part of this book may be reproduced in any form without permission in writing from the author, except in the case of brief quotations embodied in critical articles, news reports, or reviews.

Edited by Marianne Thurmond

ISBN: 979-8-5338-2994-6

Dedication

To Ed Bowman, my Dad.

God didn't send you to the jungle, but if anyone could have been a jungle missionary, it was you. You can build anything, you can fix everything, and you are a faithful teacher of God's word. Thank you for showing me how to be a hard working selfless man of God!

Also by Ernie Bowman:

Fiction

Legend of the Wapa
Jungle Missionary Series – Book 1

Non-Fiction

A Surgeon's Hands – God's Work:
The life and medical missions career of Dr. Bob Cropsey

Death is no Stranger

Ernie Bowman

1

Death is no stranger in the jungle.

It's no friend either; it's just that there is more of it here than in American life back home. My dog died when I was twelve, and I've lost one set of grandparents.

But other than that I'd had no real experience with death before coming here. I had seen many things die – every Michigan kid has. Hunting, fishing, and farming were part of life, and they all involved death at some point.

But I'm talking about death that brings personal loss. About that, I knew virtually nothing. It's not that I was uniquely ignorant – I'm guessing most people my age are the same. Life in the jungle is different; it won't let you avoid death like that.

I live with the Kilo people – an indigenous reclusive tribe in South America. Their village sits on the Brazil-Venezuela border where death is a familiar and constant reality.

Without antibiotics or modern medicine, life expectancy is somewhere south of not very good. Add to that subsistence farming, a life of manual labor, and an infant mortality rate of almost forty percent; and one death a month is the norm. Even so, the scene playing out in front of me is unusual.

Henry, the new village leader and one of my closest friends, is leading a group of men preparing a funeral pyre for his father. The duty and honor of leading the village was given to Henry by his father – on his death bed.

There has been grumbling from others who weren't chosen, but the choice was expected.

The chief has the right of naming a successor, provided he is capable of doing so prior to death. There are complicated traditions that govern the transfer of leadership, and I do not understand them all.

The declaration must be made audibly with witnesses present. The death of the outgoing leader must happen within two sunrises of his declaration. No women are ever chosen – something that would give the ACLU fits and spawn a dozen lawsuits back home, but no one in the jungle questions it.

If the village leader dies before making a declaration, or more than two sunrises pass between his declaration and his death, it's a virtual free for all. As you can imagine, that is not a pretty or a peaceful situation.

I only know this second hand, because this is the first change in leadership during our time here. The old men tell stories of fights, sabotage, and even murder. Luckily, all of that was avoided when Henry's dad chose him and then died a day later.

The death of the village leader is a big deal because it means new leadership but also because it means official mourning for the whole village. There are traditions to be observed and a ritual to be carried out, more so than with a commoner's death. The ritual takes place riverside on what might charitably be called the beach.

There's not much sand: it's mostly just a strip of land where the jungle isn't.

Strewn with rocks and patchy plants, this is one of two social hubs for the village. The other is the Commons. Where we are standing now is the waterfront. As you can see, the Kilo choose practicality over creativity with names.

Henry and the men are building what looks remarkably like a giant sized version of a child's toy log cabin. I had a set of toys when I was a kid that looked like little logs.

They came with tiny windows, miniature people, horses, and some roof panels. I loved cowboys and anything western, so the frontier toy vibe was heavy in my room. You could use the toy logs to build stuff or to throw at your brother, not that I knew anyone who would do that.

The funeral pyre they're building resembles a miniature of the cabins I made as a kid. The logs are stacked up with overlapping ends. At six feet by three feet, it is an almost perfect rectangle.

The boards and frame members from the deceased's house are interspersed throughout. The Kilo do not speak of the dead and even do their best to not remember them. At least not publicly. To that end, when a person dies their house is dismantled and burned. For the death of a village leader, those pieces of wood are always worked into the frame of a funeral pyre. It's about three feet high now and it is becoming difficult for the men to step over and into.

They call for the body.

The procession goes single file down the trail to the Waterfront. Each person is decked out in mourning regalia.

Their bodies are painted with red river clay that has dried and the effect is uncomfortably reminiscent of dried blood on cracked skin. Maybe that's the point. A mix of plants and bird feathers adorn their hair giving the procession the appearance of a walking strip of jungle.

Two men are leading, bearing a jungle hammock slung between them. Henry's dad is in the hammock. Behind the leaders come the family. Each person carries a single object.

A fire that catches quickly has been kindled inside of the pyre. Fresh cut poles are laid across the top. The body is never taken out of the hammock which is laid across the poles. One by one the people in the procession place the object they have carried onto the platform.

First goes a wooden club, then an eating bowl made from a gourd. In life these things belonged to Henry's dad. In death, they will belong to no one. An inheritance would mean reminders of the deceased, so everything is burned – clothing, tools, food, fruits, a fishing spear.

One by one, it is piled on.

The Kilo are not materialistic and have few possessions. In short order the dead man's possessions are arrayed around his body. The last thing added is a decorative arm band.

The arm band reminds me of the armband the captain of a soccer team wears during a game. Instead of elastic, this one is made of bark and feathers and is held together with vines. It is the symbol of the chief.

In soccer, if the captain has to leave the field, he passes his arm band to the man who succeeds him. Apparently that's not going to happen here.

After the household goods are added to the platform, the rest of the structure is completed. Three more layers of logs conceal the body from view. The men work quickly as the fire blazes and grows too intense to bear.

Their work completed, each man turns away, collects his family, and heads up the trail to the village. For tonight, only the family will remain.

The last of the Kilo disappear up the trail as the smoke begins to billow from the top of the pyre. I'm standing with Henry, close enough to feel the heat begin to redden my skin.

"You must go now," he says quietly.

"I can stay," I reply, already knowing what his answer will be.

"You are not at home, Ian. For you to stay with the dead is not permitted."

Henry does not know the sting of his words. But I know he means me no insult, he simply speaks the truth. We have talked about the differences between his culture and mine, about how different our ways are in almost every respect.

He listened one night, eyes bugging out of his head, as I explained the customs of autopsy and visitation before a funeral with an open casket.

The sting to my spirit doesn't come from the cultural differences though; it comes from knowing that I am not one of them – that I may never be.

Instantly, the old feeling returns. Commonly felt by foreign missionaries and high school freshmen, it is the intense sensation of not belonging.

I am acutely aware of my status here as *other*. Standing next to Henry, I almost tower over him. I'm not extremely tall – 6'1" with shoes on in the morning – but I'm six inches taller than Henry. His skin is the color of coffee. His hair looks like a charcoal sponge.

I, on the other hand, couldn't be whiter. After three years in the jungle, I have a tan; but the villagers still call me the name I was tagged with when I stepped on shore for the first time:

"Mommy!" a small child cried, hiding his face. "Is that a ghost?!"

You are not at home.

Add to my skin and height, my close cropped blond hair; and the two of us couldn't look more different if we tried. One glance and it is obvious: I am not Kilo.

I nod silently and turn to go.

Who am I then? I am Ian Allen, *Jungle Missionary*. Or so it says on my prayer letter stationery. The suit-and-tie folks at mission headquarters prefer *tribal missionary*. I like the sound of *jungle missionary* better.

I grew up in southeast Michigan, in a little town called Lapeer. My life was typical for a church kid: youth group on Wednesday, church on Sunday, try to get away with what I could in between. I was never the rebellious sort, but I liked to play the part in my head.

To be honest, my childhood was so commonplace, I was pretty much a walking Christian stereotype. When I go back to the states for speaking or fund raising, I try to turn a few heads with my standard opener:

"Good evening. For those who don't know me, my name is Ian Allen, and I'm a jungle missionary. We live on the very border of Venezuela and Brazil. Through evangelism, discipleship, and Bible translation, our goal is to plant self-sustaining churches among the Kilo people of South America."

At this point everybody has pretty much tuned out. They've heard the same spiel a hundred times from a hundred missionaries. My wife says it's petty, but I always open like that, just so their eyes will glaze over before I hit them with my punch line:

"I didn't grow up wanting to be a missionary. But God saved me from a life of drugs, alcohol, and more debauchery than I could comfortably describe for you tonight. I knew that after God saved me from such immoral living, I could do no less than give him my life in return.

"I don't normally describe details from my former life, because that's not what I want to focus on tonight.

"The plight of tribes living without access to the Word of God is infinitely more important. But I can't really tell you that story without telling you my own. So if you will permit a brief aside, I'd like to tell you how God saved me from a life of sin...."

The effect is usually as remarkable as it is predictable. The dozers are wide awake. The slouchers are sitting up straight. The pens of the doodlers have gone still.

It's somewhat disturbing how quickly people become interested in a "testimony" as soon as it involves the possibility of juicy stories. My wife is probably right and I should probably be ashamed of myself for taking advantage of it.

But I'm not.

Invariably, this gives me the undivided attention of the room as I proceed to share with them the background story of how I became a jungle missionary:

"My parents are Christians. My grandparents were Christians. My family have been Christians for generations, and I was raised in church: Sunday School, Sunday morning, and Sunday night every week, youth group on Wednesday.

"Throw in Saturday work days, mission conferences, summer revivals, and any other church gathering you can print in a bulletin – we had them all.

"This didn't make me a perfect kid by any means, but I wasn't as depraved as I could have been. Yes, the Lord saved me from a desperately immoral life.

"And he did so by giving me loving Christian parents who taught me right from wrong and brought me up to know him and to love him. I was born again as a young child and I've been more-or-less faithful to Christ since then."

At this point, I've lost many of them.

They feel tricked and they don't appreciate it.

Never mind that they should be ashamed of getting interested only when their ears were tickled by the possibility of sin, because that's a whole other story.

Nonetheless, a certain percentage of the people listening have tuned out, but I don't care.

I don't go around speaking for just anyone.

I speak for the people still paying attention, the people like me: church lifers looking for more.

The truth is, if a person is content with the life they're living, I don't have much for them. The work we're doing is not a casual commitment for the faint of heart.

"When I was in 11th grade, our youth group visited a training site for foreign missionaries – but not just any foreign missionaries – tribal missionaries who go where no one else has been. There are over two thousand people groups in the world that have never heard the gospel. I saw six different churches in town today, but there are millions of people in the world with no idea about Jesus. That week in Pennsylvania I heard about those people groups. I learned about pioneer missionaries – John Patton, Paul Dye, and Paul Flemming.

"They were men who hiked into the jungle with just the clothes on their backs and the tools they could carry on a donkey. I heard stories about great sacrifices for God, stories of adventure that made Indiana Jones look like a fairy tale princess! And I knew…that's what I wanted. I wanted to be a jungle missionary! I wanted to hike with natives and build air strips. I wanted to meet a tribe with no alphabet and help them write one. I wanted to teach them about God and tell them about Jesus.

"I wanted to see the first edition of a new Bible roll off the presses in a language no other white man on earth could read. I wanted to be a jungle missionary, and I wanted to live in a tree house like the Swiss Family Robinson!"

At this point in the speech I've lost about half of the remaining listeners I had, even if they do chuckle politely at my lame jokes.

Most of the adults have stopped listening, and that's okay. I've got the attention of the young people now, the ones who dream of exotic adventure.

That's who I speak for. That's who will come join us in the jungle and live through days like today, days where people die without hope and motivate us to work harder. It's not that adults don't care; I know they do.

But this work is not for old people.

It takes time – an estimated eight to ten years from the day we arrive to the day that Bible rolls off the presses. Old people don't have that kind of time, so I gear my talks to the young.

I go heavy on the jungle stories with emphasis on adventure. I've got machetes to show and drinking gourds to pick up and pass around.

On my next trip home, I'm hoping to bring Henry with me, a living breathing example of the work's importance. For now though, I'm here with him, where I am "not at home."

I walk the path to the village with my wife Rachael. We go hand-in-hand, something the Kilo would never do. Generations of experience walking narrow paths have ingrained patterns in their minds. Those patterns don't change when they walk the one path wide enough to hold hands on.

So as I look ahead to the group further along, I see them walking in single file on the left hand side of the path, jungle style.

I think about those recruiting trips back home as we walk, savoring the feel of her hand in mine.

The nature of the work here means that we spend more time together than most couples back home, but rarely do we walk hand-in-hand. Sometimes it's the small things that make life better. Actually, check that. Jungle life teaches you really quickly that it is *always* the small things that make life better. Life is made of small things.

The truth is, sometimes I feel bad about the picture I paint of life as a jungle missionary. It's not all adventure and jaguar stalks, although I do have a really great story about a hunting trip like that. Several months ago a near-mythical animal called a Wapa came to the area around the village.

The Wapa is a sacred animal to the Kilo, but the history is such that whenever one comes around, it has to be hunted and killed. Don't ask me to explain the *Legend of the Wapa* right now – it would take a book to do it!

Suffice to say, the hunt was a success despite the fact that I had to sew a man's toe back onto his foot in the middle of the jungle and he almost died.

Like I said, it's a long story.

Right now I don't have time to tell it because Rachael and I are walking up to our house. It's a ranch style house with a covered front porch and a storage shed out back for tools and fishing spears. What? You don't keep fishing spears in your garden shed?

Welcome to life in the jungle!

There's no garage, because we don't own a car – there are no roads. There is only the river, the trails, and the airstrip we built by hand. What? You don't have a private air strip?

Welcome to life in the jungle!

The village itself is typical for the Kilo people, but I don't even know why I use that phrase.

I've only ever seen two Kilo villages, ours and one other, so I don't know how typical it can be. I'm told there are more "in the south" but it takes so long to walk there that we have never made an attempt.

My house backs up to the jungle itself, and supposedly the actual border of Brazil-Venezuela runs right through my house. Funny thing though, the Brazilian jungle in the back yard looks just like the Venezuelan jungle in front!

Standing on my porch and looking left, you can see part of the airstrip fifty yards down the trail. There is another major trail that runs at a right angle off the airstrip and into the jungle. Kitty-corner to the right is the home of Jeff and Wendy Williams, our best friends and missionary partners.

Our houses look alike because we built them the same – Jeff and I together, working with a small team of guys from our home churches. It was a month of men camping in the jungle and building houses by hand. I've never been more tired in my life, but we were motivated by conviction and need – two of the best motivators you can find!

Down the lane to the right, you'll find the village proper. There are several rings of homes in a semi-circle, each constructed by hand out of jungle materials. With no home improvement store around to get nails and no lumberyard for plywood, the Kilo make do with what they have.

All things considered, they're doing just fine.

The Commons is like the town square – a public area where the meeting house for public business is located.

The village takes up less than a half square mile and has about two hundred people in total, not counting the missionaries.

Trails lead off from the Commons into the undergrowth. A hundred yards beyond the tree line is the area where gardens are cleared and kept, and that's basically it. There isn't much to the village itself, or really to life in the jungle. All of this passes through my mind as I look out from my porch, wondering what to do next.

The funeral rites dictate that no one leave home tonight, while the body of the deceased leader burns.

The Kilo have returned to their homes and the village is quiet. In an old western, there would be a grim faced cowpoke to declare things *"too quiet."*

But it's not a western and there are no cowpokes. It's just me and the quiet of the village. Twilight is descending and soon I'll be able to see the glow of the funeral pyre burning.

I look over at the Williams' house and see Jeff on his porch. He looks a question over at me, raising his eyebrows to indicate as much.

What passes between us is as good as a conversation, though no actual words are exchanged:

Jeff, holding up a deck of cards: *Want to have dinner and play cards?*

Me, shrugging my shoulders and nodding in the direction of the funeral fire: *Should we? We're supposed to stay inside, right?*

Jeff, holding his hands out in a "what-can-you-do?" gesture, looking side-to-side: *Why not? There's nobody around.*

I briefly hold up one finger and duck back inside the house to check if Rachael has already started dinner.

"Hey Babe, have you started dinner yet? Jeff wants to know if we want to hang out with them."

"Sure. I have some pork chops for you to grill, but I just thawed them today, so they'll keep until tomorrow."

Rachael is a gift from God. How else do you explain a woman who is godly, selfless, way too good looking for me, has a smile that melts the coldest of hearts, and is willing to trek off and live in the jungle?

As I step back out to give Jeff a silent thumbs up, she wraps the chops and puts them quickly into the fridge. Two Cokes go in as well and I'm emphasizing the "quickly" part of this because our refrigerator is – how can I put this nicely?

Old. We have an old refrigerator.

But it was free and it works – eventually.

You just have to give it time.

It's rather like the hand-me-down car I had when I was sixteen. The car ran okay, but if you insisted on accelerating at anything resembling a brisk pace, it simply refused. Zero to sixty in a minute? More like zero to sixty in an hour.

I'm exaggerating of course, but only slightly.

The car forced you to take your time and go slow because it took its time and went slow – sort of like our old fridge.

Given that, we try to open the fridge as little as possible.

If you open the fridge a bunch of times and let in warm air, you'll have lukewarm milk for dinner. Once it's down to the correct temperature, it does fine. It just takes its sweet ole' time getting there, just like that old car.

That's why Rachael is quick about putting the chops in and why she does double duty with the Cokes. The Coke is for this weekend. Sunday is football day – one of my weekly rituals, even in the jungle.

Stepping out and softly closing the door, we glance both ways and scoot across. Jeff holds the door and we sneak inside. I glance back over my shoulder as we do, and I feel utterly ridiculous.

Darting inside so no one sees us. I

Closing the door ever-so-quietly.

Sneaking around the house

It's like we're teenagers coming home late for curfew.

But we're not teenagers trying to steal a few kisses, we're adult missionaries having dinner with friends.

So why all the cloak and dagger stuff?

Missionary life is a constant balancing act.

On the one hand, we're careful not to do anything that would upset our Kilo hosts. The gospel itself is inherently offensive enough. Because of that we don't want to cause any unnecessary offense that could set the work back significantly.

Depending on the offense, it might even jeopardize the work altogether.

Missionary history is full of horror stories about outsiders blundering into a foreign culture willy-nilly. Some of them offended the native population so badly that no one wanted anything to do with them at all. We don't want to be that guy, so we do our best to be inoffensive when we can.

On the other hand, we can't be held completely hostage to local customs. As Henry painfully reminded me this evening, we are not Kilo. We are trying to assimilate as best we can, but it will never be seamless. The balancing act is in trying to figure out which cultural practices we can ignore and which we need to respect.

Food is a good example. We eat some of the things the Kilo eat. I have learned to spear and eat fish, and the taste is growing on me. Before coming here, if I ate fish it had to be battered and fried. Now though, I'm becoming accustomed to fish on a regular basis, simply because eating it makes me more approachable to the Kilo.

In other ways though, we remain distinctly American. Have you ever thought about how weird drinking milk is? Of course not.

But here, the only people who drink milk are nursing babies. Given that, try explaining to someone who has never seen a cow, exactly what that glass full of white stuff is.

No really – go ahead and think about it. How would you explain it?

I had no idea either.

I tried to explain what a cow was.

That went nowhere fast.

I tried explaining where milk comes from. I saw some recognition, but no understanding. Suckling pigs and nursing babies they understood. But grownups drinking it by the glassful? Not so much.

Eventually, the best we came up with was "female animal liquid." Yup, that was the best I had. To this day the Kilo think it's gross and they won't touch milk. I tried to get them to taste it, but once something has been dubbed "female animal liquid," there's no recovering from that!

So in regards to drinking milk, we remain very American. Same thing with peanut butter. What's wrong with peanut butter, you ask? Just think about it for a minute and you'll get it. Picture a scoop of peanut butter sitting on a plate (I eat it right out of the jar by the spoonful). Got the image in your head? Now imagine what that might remind a jungle tribesman of when he saw it for the first time, having never seen a peanut.

I just ruined peanut butter for you, didn't I? You're welcome.

Sometimes we conform to the Kilo culture, and sometimes we don't.

There's no rule book for when to do which. Food goes easily in the "okay not to conform" column.

We're not sure yet about customs for mourning the death of a tribal leader.

Because it's a potentially touchy subject, we close the blinds and draw the curtains. Dinner smells like baked pasta and garlic bread, but I'll have to wait until Wendy comes inside to confirm that.

The one thing we can't generate enough electricity to run is an air conditioner. Because of this, Jeff and I built some outdoor ovens.

They stand just off the back porch and are made of bricks and are fired by wood. They aren't fancy but they keep the heat out of the house.

If my description sounds like something from an *Outdoor Living* magazine to you, you have clearly never had the misfortune to behold our masonry work. Jeff and I make the bricks ourselves and the result is predictable. The ovens need regular upkeep – about one new brick a month – but it's still pretty cool that we made our own ovens!

I read this quote from Picasso: "I am always doing that which I cannot do, in order that I may learn how to do it," which sums up life for me pretty well.

With no hardware store and no handy-man service, I've become a jack-of-all-trades-master-of-none out of necessity.

If I want something built, I build it myself. If I want something fixed, I fix it myself. In many ways, it's like living a boyhood dream.

I spent history class in elementary school staring out the window and wondering what it would be like to cross the country as a pioneer and build a little house on the prairie.

My imaginary adventures were infinitely more interesting than the dates being written on the blackboard; that's for sure!

Being a jungle missionary is like that from time to time. We're pioneers of a different sort.

"So what's up with this 'everybody inside for the night' thing?" Jeff asks.

"I'm not sure," I reply. "Something to do with the transfer of leadership. Henry is with his dad's body, but everyone else is expected to stay home."

"Is this a rational thing, or a spiritual thing?"

Jeff's question is not as offensive as it might seem. He's not making fun of the spiritual beliefs of the Kilo or implying that spiritual faith is irrational. The Kilo are an extremely rational and pragmatic people. The jungle forces them to be. If something doesn't serve a practical purpose they won't bother with it, no matter how insensitive or socially awkward it might seem to outsiders.

Clothes are one example.

Clothes are difficult to make by hand so the Kilo wear as little as necessary. And by "necessary," I do not mean to imply that a certain standard of decency must be met.

They wear clothes only if they serve a functional purpose at the moment. Physical modesty is not one of those purposes. The lone exception to their ruthless pragmatism is their spirituality.

The Kilo will go to great and costly lengths to gain spiritual benefit.

Their religion holds that everything with lungs has a spirit. Those spirits can be summoned and co-opted by spiritually attune people, and not always for good purposes.

This being the case, Kilo shamans will go to great lengths to curry favor with certain spirits. Jeff was asking if this is one of those cases.

"I think it's a rational thing," I tell him. "It seems related to the fact that a successor was named."

"It sounds like a curfew to prevent mischief," Rachael says. "Which makes sense, I guess. The new leader will never be more vulnerable than he is right now."

"Who's vulnerable?" asks Wendy, coming through the back door holding a steaming dish.

"We're talking about the curfew," Jeff tells her.

"Right," she says. "I thought that was kind of weird."

"Me too," Jeff replies. "We're trying to figure out why they might have it. Best guess so far is to protect the new leader from rivals until he can establish himself."

"Yeah, well, right now, I think you need to be worried about protecting the garlic bread from burning," she says. "It's still in the oven. Can you get it please?"

"Now there's a woman with her priorities straight!" Jeff says, ducking out the back door.

Dinner isn't just pasta and garlic bread – it's lasagna and garlic bread. Wendy had found a package of sausage buried in the bottom of the small chest freezer our families share, along with a rare bag of mozzarella cheese.

I say "rare" because Jeff *really* likes cheese and it never lasts long at their house. Wendy had hidden the bag of cheese on the bottom and forgot about it.

Dinner is delicious as usual. I may be biased, but I swear baking your food in a wood fired oven makes it taste better.

On the rare occasions we use the propane oven in the house, it just doesn't taste the same. The lasagna has a smoky flavor that is just fantastic. A food magazine would call it "authentic" or "transportive" or some other such thing.

An hour later, as I'm dealing out the last hand of euchre' – guys against girls, just like Children's Church – I'm struck by how different my missionary life is from the religion of my childhood.

Movies were evil, dancing was unthinkable, and playing cards was forbidden. They were all considered "worldly."

And yet, here we are as missionaries, playing cards. It makes me wonder which of *our* closely held religious practices from today will be discarded as outdated by the next generation.

It's not an idle question either.

As pioneer missionaries on a new field we are forced to make these distinctions about a variety of issues.

For example: do you have to have grape juice or wine to properly observe Communion? There are no grapes here, but there's plenty of other fruit. We'll have to deal with that soon enough, as a Kilo church is planted.

For now, Jeff and I win the euchre' game by a bare point, a result that is closer than we typically have. We say our goodbyes, glance both ways, and scoot across the lane.

Quickly onto our own porch, we're inside and away from the potentially prying eyes of curious Kilo.

Again, I feel ridiculous. But until we can sort out which category funeral customs belong in, this is the way it has to be.

We go through the nighttime routines of couples the world over.

Teeth are brushed and alarm clocks are set.

The coffee pot is put on delayed brew, and we climb into bed to say goodnight.

I typically read for an hour while Rachael falls right to sleep.

It might be very unmissionary-like, but at night I read fiction – mostly detective novels or spy thrillers.

I read plenty of theology and mission theory during the work day, but nights are strictly for fiction. Sometimes it backfires because I get involved in a story and stay awake way longer than I should. Tonight is not one of those nights.

I'm trying out a new author and it's not working. I'm sure he's a nice guy, but his story telling needs help.

He's a bit too gratuitous with the violence for my tastes. The bad guy needs to be shot in the end, but I don't want my nose rubbed in the blood.

Little did I know how violent the coming days would turn out to be.

I click off my reading light, rearrange the pillow, and lay there in the dark thinking about my day.

The elaborate funeral rites stand out against the sheer ordinariness of dinner and cards at a friend's house. This mixing of the exotic and the ordinary is typical for life as a jungle missionary. In so many ways my life is like anyone else's.

I get up, go to work, eat dinner, and hang out with friends. Other times though?

Not so much.

Any given day can bring twists unknown to life in "civilized" society. Jungle hunts, spear fishing, and today, ritual cremation.

Truth be told though, the ordinary days far outnumber the absurd ones.

That's fine with me because my personality is a bit habitual and I thrive on routine. I have a deep need for consistency in life and work.

This, along with a fierce independent streak, have combined to make me into what one of my missionary trainers once described as "almost the ideal tribal missionary."

My biggest weakness in his eyes? I don't like fish.

Being a jungle missionary sounds exotic, because it is. It's also hard. But if you can work hard you can do what I do.

Plenty of people think they could never do what I do. It sounds exotic and impossible to be a jungle missionary, but seriously – I'm no one special.

Just ask Jeff.

Like any good friend, he'll be happy to tell you how very un-special I am!

Learning an unknown language, creating an alphabet, teaching the people to read their own language (from an alphabet you created!), translating the Bible so they can read it, evangelizing a primitive tribe, and starting a church may sound like a crazy-out-there-never-going-to-happen thing, but it's not.

In all honesty, if I can do it, anyone can. The only thing stopping you from doing the same thing is *work*.

This is what I fall asleep thinking about: work. In the morning I plan to translate the latest list of verbs Henry recorded for me. It won't make for an exciting story, but hopefully it *will* make for an accurate Bible and – one day – a faithful Kilo church!

2

The morning dawns bright and clear – same as usual.

Did you ever hear one of those country songs on the radio about life at the beach and how great it is to wake up in paradise? Yeah well, that's my life.

I stand on the back porch and sip coffee.

The sun is poking over the trees, casting shadows across my house.

The mist hangs just over the treetops and the effect is stunning and picturesque.

I'm still rubbing the sleepy gunk out of my eyes but the birds have been up for hours. They swoop over the river for food.

Watching them dive from the fog and through the mist is like living in a nature documentary. The colors are incredible and multiple species are on full display.

The Kilo are early risers, and the women have already left the village for the gardens. Children are out in force, darting from one place to another.

Like kids everywhere, they seem to have no ability to walk. They run, they dash, and they sprint; but they never walk.

I finish my coffee and clean up the breakfast dishes while Rachael goes to get ready for the day. She wears almost no make-up, but takes a lot of care in doing her hair which, believe it or not, is the norm here.

Kilo women take pains at making up their appearance, although outside observers can be forgiven for not thinking so.

There is a particular jungle plant that grows by the river that is prized for its look. The women all have pierced ears, and a common beauty practice is to string a thread of bark from one lobe to the other, passing under the chin in a loose loop.

They string the bark necklace with these leaves (*shtuverblub* they call the plant), spaced apart by the inedible berries that grow in clusters at its base. The alternating green leaves and red berries give off a Christmas-like vibe reminiscent of holly wreaths.

On special occasions, women will weave the stems and leaves of this plant through their hair. It's a rather involved process usually reserved for big days. A birth, a death, giving a child away as a bride, or other social events that call for ceremony and formality call for *shtuverblub*.

It seems that no matter where you go on this earth, you'll find people trying to make themselves look different than they are.

There's a sermon illustration in there somewhere – maybe I'll mine it out later on. Pondering these peculiarities of life, I sit down at my home office and boot up the laptop.

I turn on the tape recorder and plug in the headphones, slipping them over my ears. Arrayed on the table in front of me are pictures numbered from one to twenty-three.

I'm a visual learner, and I've developed a system for learning verbs. I struggle to finger paint but Rachael is an excellent artist. She will draw a picture of a common activity: a person fishing, a child running, or a man chopping wood.

I show the pictures to Henry who gives me the Kilo word for each. He repeats them slowly into my recorder, carefully enunciating each syllable. As he does this, I number the pictures and lay them on the table in order, careful not to mix them up.

This process gives me a corresponding visual for each word on the tape. I can then go back and translate them at my own pace. As I work, I update our growing Kilo language database.

This is the tedious part of the job that I was telling you about before.

Probably half my time is spent right here in the office, either with Henry and the recorder, or with the database in translation work.

The other half of my time is spent in the village, learning the language and customs of the people. There's no class for it and no textbook to follow. I carry a little notebook to jot things down so I can remember what I learn.

There is no substitute for this type of first hand cultural education. Some things you just can't learn in a classroom.

The morning creeps by and I have to really concentrate to stay focused. Every time someone walks by outside I glance up, hoping to see Henry. I don't need him for the work today; I just want to know what is happening. I see no men out and about today – only women and children.

Hours pass with no sign of Henry. Rachael spends the morning writing to our supporters back home.

We have an update sheet that goes out once a month and we try to add a personal touch to each one. She finishes up the letter she's working on and asks if I want lunch.

"No," I say, standing up and stretching. "I'm not hungry. I think I'll just head out and see if I can talk to anyone."

"Okay, but if you change your mind there's some trail mix on the counter."

Trail mix is my go-to midday food, but with the exception of raisins, it isn't like the trail mix from back home. M&M's are impossible to find down here, so we use chocolate chips instead. Peanuts are likewise completely scarce, but we've found a substitute.

There is a nut bearing tree here called *schstufferbleg*. The nuts are about the size of a small almond and slightly bitter. They go well with the chocolate chips. Throw in some raisins and granola and that's what I eat for lunch most days, heavy on the raisins.

I open the bag and grab a handful, kissing Rachael on the cheek in the process. She smiles and says:

"I thought you weren't hungry?"

"I'm not," I mumble through a mouthful of food.

"That's disgusting – don't talk with your mouth full."

Her smile is gone, replaced by mine.

"Okay, Mom." I say with a grin that she doesn't return.

She hates it when I say that, and I don't know why I still do sometimes.

Teasing girls for scraps of attention is supposed to end in junior high. Shaking my head, I turn to go outside, mentally pausing long enough to reflect on my spiritual maturity level today.

The people back home treat me with this detached aura of missionary respect; and here I am, reverting to fourth grade flirting rituals. If they only knew.

I tuck a water bottle into my back pocket and close the door as I leave, careful not to let it slam behind me. Rachael hates that too, and I figure I've irritated her enough for one lifetime.

Swallowing the last of the trail mix, I glance around as I step off the porch. It looks like a ghost town; a tumbleweed would complete the picture. There's one old lady shuffling away from Jeff's house, a mangy looking dog following on her heels.

Two kids are squatting together by the tree line. They seem to be sharing some type of food. They take turns picking off a large leaf on the ground between them, bringing it to their lips. Probably roasted grubs or something. I'm not kidding.

Guessing that the action is happening down at the river, I turn left.

The path continues for a bit until it comes to the airstrip we cleared by hand – all two hundred yards of it. Yes, it was just as difficult as it sounds, but totally worth it.

A month of chopping, digging, hauling, clearing, and burning gave us a huge advantage. Without that airstrip, the initial work of establishing a mission base here would have taken an additional two years.

A plane from the mission aviation base can bring in three times as much stuff, three times as fast as a boat could.

The rapids and sandbars on the river make it impossible to bring more than a dozen tubs worth of stuff to the village at a time. Everything has to be taken out of the boat and portaged overland whenever the river becomes impassable, not something you want to do on a regular basis. It's much easier to fly it in by plane.

The village path ends at the airstrip, and the path to the river branches off the end. To the left there is a hundred yards of airstrip, then a million square miles of jungle beyond that. Looking down the length of the airstrip, I see a lone figure almost all the way down. At this distance, I can tell for sure that it's a Kilo man, but not much else. Deciding against going to the waterfront, I turn that way and walk down the edge of the airstrip.

I'm careful to stay in the shadows and out of the burning sun. As I draw nearer, I can see the man has a machete and is hacking at the encroaching jungle.

Coming closer I can finally make out who it is – Henry!

"*Shmeekee!*" I call out, raising an open hand straight up.

This is the common way of calling out to a friend at a distance. There are various ways of hailing or addressing someone in Kilo culture, each specific to the situation. The English variation that comes closest to "Shmeekee!" is probably the nautical greeting of "Ahoy!"

It gets the person's attention, while at the same time indicating peaceful intent. Most often it's a greeting from a boat approaching shore or a visitor approaching the village unannounced.

Hearing my greeting, Henry looks up from his work and raises his own arm straight up. The open palm indicates a welcome reception.

A raised fist would have meant something else.

Seeing the open palm I cut across the airstrip, feeling the heat of the sun as I leave the shade of the trees beside me.

"Henry, what are you doing out here?"

"Working on my garden!" he says with a grin.

That doesn't make any sense but must be true, since sarcasm is unknown to the Kilo culture. "Weak words without the strength of truth" they said when I explained the English phenomenon.

Quite so, I thought – there's probably a sermon illustration in that quote somewhere too. At any rate, Henry learned quickly and he's even come to use sarcasm himself sometimes when talking to us. I'm not sure that's a good thing.

"Funny," I say. "But really, what are you doing?"

"I am not using weak words." His smile has disappeared. "This," indicating the airstrip, "is to be my privilege garden."

"What? You know you can't plant here."

"You do not understand."

Clearly I was missing something.

The privilege garden is a plot of land used exclusively by the chief. But he doesn't tend it, the villagers do. It's like a salary of food, paid by taxes of hours worked in the garden.

"Isn't there already a privilege garden?"

Henry sees my water bottle and motions toward it, indicating a request for a drink. I unscrew the cap and hand it over, watching as he drains almost all of it without coming up for a breath.

Watching this I am certain he would have won the chugging contests we had in the school cafeteria growing up!

Finally taking the bottle from his lips, he wipes his mouth with the back of his hand and looks down the airstrip toward the river.

"That was my father's," he says with sadness and admiration. "For three hands he was leader. Now he is gone. Before the sun today, I buried his bones and cut down his garden. We will use it no more."

Out of respect for his father he won't look at me as he speaks.

The Kilo never speak of the dead unless it is absolutely necessary, and then only in euphemisms.

For Henry to speak so directly about his dead father is highly unusual. Sensing the unique situation, I gently probe for more insight."

"Is that the usual way?"

"Yes. We bury the bones of a leader in his garden and abandon it to the jungle, as he has been abandoned to the spirits." He voice is sad but resolute as he gazes into the middle distance, not meeting my eyes.

"But how can *this* be your garden?"

Slowly and softly, he explains. He tells me of customs and practices I have yet to hear spoken out loud. These are things the Kilo do not speak of openly.

When he finishes, Henry has spoken more words to me than he would normally use in a week of regular life.

Clearly this is not a regular time of life.

Each village leader is marked by an armband of leather, bark, and feathers. He wears it at ceremonial times of village life. Upon the death of one leader and the declaration of another, the dead leader is cremated in a funeral pyre – with his armband – and his bones are buried in his privilege garden by the newly chosen leader.

The garden site is cleared of growth and abandoned. Anything growing in the garden at the time is buried along with the leader's bones. It belongs to the jungle and the spirits now.

The new leader works alone, on the morning after the cremation, while the men of the village go off into the jungle, one by one. They each have a choice: will they follow the new leader, or go their own way?

If a man chooses not to follow the new chief, he must leave. He must make his way into the jungle, possibly to another Kilo village, if one is known. Dissent is not tolerated, debate is not entertained. The only other option is armed revolt which Henry tells me thankfully that he has never seen.

The men who submit to the new chief go hunting by themselves.

Solo hunting is almost unheard of for the Kilo, because the jungle is dangerous and a successful trip usually requires cooperation. But on this occasion, they hunt alone.

When the hunters leave for the jungle, the new chief leader leaves to complete his tasks in the privilege garden.

When he completes the job of demolishing it and burying his predecessor, he has two tasks of his own. He must make an armband, and he must carve out a new privilege garden.

"Wait a minute," I interrupt. "I thought the chief never worked his own garden."

"That is true. But only after it is completed."

"So *he* creates his garden, but *the people* work it for him?"

"The people will help to create it. But yes, that is correct." His voice is so quiet I can barely hear him. I feel bad and silently vow not to interrupt again.

Henry explains that once the new chief has his arm band in place, he begins to clear a garden for himself. At this point he *is* the leader, but a leader of no one in particular.

"He has a bare arm," Henry says by way of explanation, indicating his own arm.

For the first time I notice he is wearing an arm band that is, well....bare.

It is nothing but a wrap of uncured leather around his upper arm. There are dozens of slits in it all the way around.

This conversation with Henry is the first I have heard of how the chief gains his armband.

As the new leader works to clear his own privilege garden, the men of the village are hunting. As each man finds success in the hunt – hopefully by killing a Macaw – they pluck and roast it, eating by themselves in the jungle.

Large feathers are a valuable commodity used for all kinds of things. The colorful ones are prized the most, which is why a Macaw is preferred. But when the men return from this particular hunt, they do not take their prizes back to the village. They find the chief in his new garden and present him with the feathers, wrapped in a banana leaf.

Each man then selects one feather: the most colorful, the longest, the flashiest. He places the feather into a slit of the chief's arm band and joins him in the work of clearing the garden. By these three acts: offering the feathers from his kill, inserting one into the armband, and helping to clear the privilege garden, a man signifies his willingness to follow the new chief.

The burying of the old leader and the hunt for Macaw typically take the morning, which means the new leader must have his garden site chosen and begun to work by noon.

Henry pauses for a full minute. I wait expectantly, but I get the sense that he is done talking. I don't feel bad about speaking, because now I'm not interrupting:

"What happens if the men come back, but no site has been chosen for the garden, and no work has been done?"

"I cannot say," Henry replies, still looking off down the airstrip.

"It has never happened. It will not happen."

"Why here, Henry? It's not much of a garden."

"It is no garden at all. The garden is merely a symbol of the man himself. What is important is that it *is*." He emphasizes the last word like a philosophy professor.

"I don't understand."

"You will."

At this point I'm a little frustrated. Since day one, Henry has been more than a neighbor to me. He has been my friend. He has gone out of his way to help me. He has taken great care, at significant personal cost, to make sure I learn what I need to know. Unlike some of the others, he has never taken pleasure in feeding me wrong information.

When we first came, I quickly learned the phrase *"Chi wadan?"* which meant *"What is it?"* I asked anyone who would talk to me, over-and-over; *Chi wadan?*

But I noticed that some of them would snicker and laugh. Once I pointed to a bow and arrow and asked: *Chi wadan?* But when I asked to borrow one man's bow and arrow – a common thing among friends – he became angry and made indications to fight.

I was saved when Henry heard the commotion and intervened. When tempers cooled I noticed men laughing off to the side. One of them was the man who taught me how to say "bow and arrow." Turns out, he gave me the word for "favorite wife."

No wonder I almost started a fight.

Others did similar things, but never Henry.

He didn't take advantage of my ignorance for his own amusement.

He had always treated me with kindness and patience – which is part of what made his silence right now so infuriating.

Why won't he talk to me? I know he just lost his dad, but I'm dying for information!

I'm just about to vent some frustration to him when he begins to speak again quietly. Startlingly, he looks directly at me.

"The garden is a symbol. Where it is, how big it is, and even what grows in it are all of no matter. What matters is that I have a garden, and that the men agree to build it with me.

"The garden was chosen as a symbol of leadership because it signifies what is most important: food. To me, food is not most important. *Kaale'* is most important. The airstrip brought us *Kaale'*, so *this* will be my garden."

At first I don't get it. *Kaale'* is the Kilo word meaning "big God."

The English equivalent would be "our Heavenly Father."

Here in the village, the Bible is the word of *Kaale'*. When we pray we "commune with *Kaale'*."

Realization lands with a thud, and it hits me.

I know what Henry's doing, and I'm stunned.

"The word of *Kaale'* came through the airstrip," I begin, pretty much thinking out loud. "The chief's privilege garden is a statement of what is most important. By making the airstrip your garden, you are saying the word of *Kaale'* is the more important – your food will be here."

"You still do not understand."

"Then help me understand!" I blurt. I'm frustrated, obviously. But I'm also excited because I feel like Henry is onto something big here.

"My garden will not be here. The *airstrip* will be my garden. He says "airstrip" with exaggerated emphasis again, looking at me expectantly. Clearly he hopes that I am picking up what he thinks he is so obviously laying down.

"Wait – you won't be planting a garden at all! You chose the airstrip *as* your garden, and the people will be working for you on the airstrip itself, to keep it up and keep it cleared?"

"Now you understand," he says, finally turning his gaze away.

I am speechless – truly speechless.

What Henry has done is not only unprecedented, it's unthinkable.

He just made an official declaration that the entire village will actively support the missionary work of Kaale'.

My eyes aren't focused on any one thing as my brain scrambles, trying to make sense of what to think of all this.

My initial reaction is shock.

But five seconds after the shock wears off, I start to see problems – nothing but problems.

What if the people don't want to work in *Kaale's* cause?

What if this precipitates social conflict?

What if Henry's family won't have enough to eat without a garden?

What if...

"Henry," I say, focusing on him as he stares resolutely down the airstrip, "are you sure this is the right thing to do?"

"Right or wrong, who can say? But it is."

Since when did he become such a philosopher? I can't decide if that sounds like the most contented thing I've ever heard, or like a Chinese takeout fortune cookie.

"Maybe you should think this through," I say. "You might want to move your garden to...." I hesitate, unsure of what I'm trying to say "...to an actual garden?"

"There is no time. It is, and it is too late."

His gaze is still directed down the runway, but it is no longer unfocused. I turn to see what has captured his attention. A man is emerging from the village trail.

"Right or wrong," Henry whispers, "we will see what the people's verdict is."

3

"You must go now." Henry says. "What comes next is only for Kilo. If the others come and see you, they may think this was your idea."

"What would happen then?" I ask stupidly, not understanding the gravity of the situation.

"Nothing good – now *go*."

I slip into the jungle on a game trail leading toward the end of the airstrip. I don't understand everything, but that's okay. Being surrounded by strange things on a daily basis, I have learned to be okay with not knowing.

Not knowing why a group of children is laughing at me. Not knowing why I am invited to some hunts, but not others. And today, not knowing why being seen with Henry would be bad.

I want to be there for Henry right now. I want to help. I want to explain. I want to pick up a machete and work by his side. I want the whole tribe to know I stand behind Henry's leadership.

But right now I have to concentrate on where I'm going. It's easy to get lost in the jungle, even when relatively close to the village. The trail I'm following is old and grown over. It twists and turns around large trees, running generally parallel to the airstrip. At the end there is a path winding back to the village, coming around the back of the Commons.

I lose the trail at one point and have to back track to a large tree I remember going around, but eventually it meets up with the larger one running across it.

I take it, wondering what time it is and when I'll be able to see Henry again. In a few minutes I see the outskirts of the village after rounding the last bend.

I break into the open ground and pause to look around. There are no men – only a handful of children and old women. At this point of the day, most of the women are out tending their gardens.

Thinking of gardens makes me wonder again about Henry's decision. Jeff and I will have to talk it over. Up to this point, keeping up the airstrip has been the job of the missionaries. We built it. We use it. We maintain it. The men help, but it has always been our responsibility. Plus, we always paid the guys who did work for us.

The Kilo have been happy to work for us on the airstrip in exchange for a variety of items because of their novelty and their usefulness: machetes, tools, or food.

A metal garden hoe is far superior to one made of wood hardened over a fire. But now, the simple act of helping the missionaries has become a political question.

I'm not certain I want our missionary work to have political overtones. No, check that, I am *absolutely* certain I do not want our missionary work to have political overtones.

I hate it when pastors turn their pulpits into campaign stops, and I won't like it any better if it happens here.

As I'm getting good and worked up over this, my heart almost stops as a woman's scream rips through the village!

My blood pressure spikes and I instinctively turn toward the sound of the scream, just as it hits again.

I have no idea what is happening, but I'm running to find out.

There's a woman in painful trouble and a thought hits me: the men are gone – it's just me and Jeff right now.

I'm sprinting through the village, the close packed houses a blur on the sides as I frantically search for the source of the sound. I'm beginning to wonder if I'm not too late – has she already been killed? – when I round a corner and stop dead in my tracks. Or to be more precise, someone stops me dead in my tracks.

Smacking into another running body, we tumble to the ground. In the tangle of legs and the violence of the fall, I see flashes of white skin. I land in a heap on top of Jeff, my elbow in his ear and his foot on my chest. Untangling ourselves from the world's worst game of Twister, we try to speak at the same time. But with the wind knocked out of you, it's hard to do anything but gasp.

"What was……....…..I heard……....…is she……....…?" I eke out between ragged half-breaths. The exertion of running full bore, plus the impact of our collision, has left me pretty much unable to communicate.

For his part, Jeff isn't doing much better. He scrambles to his feet and tries to speak but quickly gives up. Bending at the waist and leaning his hands on his knees, he holds up one finger in a "wait-a-minute" gesture.

We both catch our breath. He finds his voice first.

"What was that? Did you hear those screams?"
"How could I not?"
"Why did they stop?"

It's been a full minute since the last scream. An eerie quiet has settled over the village. Even the birds have gone still in the noise vacuum created by the retreating sound.

"I don't know, but I hope –" I start to reply, but I'm cut off by another scream.

This one is louder and worse.

Without a word, we both sprint in the direction of the scream – around a corner to our right. Jeff is faster and he turns the corner first, but I'm right behind.

For the second time in as many minutes, I run smack into Jeff at full speed. He has stopped in the lane, just around the corner of the nearest house.

We manage to keep our feet this time, but not by much. Another scream pieces the air and a woman with a water gourd hurries into a nearby hut. Instantly, I know what's happening.

"A baby," I say, peering over Jeff's shoulder. The woman disappears into the house. The banana leaf curtain door flops closed behind her.

"I thought it was a raid," he says by way of reply.

"Me too. And with the men gone, I don't know what we would have done."

Pillaging raids from other tribes are rare but not entirely unheard of, not because our nearest neighbors are so nice, but because it's almost a month's hike to get here.

Even still, the village keeps a guard up. Jeff was thinking what I was thinking. Luckily for us – if not for the woman in question – the screams were cries of labor pain, not assault by marauders.

"Welp, I suppose we'll have no part in this!" Jeff says with a little grin.

His smile is equal parts relief and genuine good humor. The Kilo would be astonished to know that in America an expectant father often accompanies his wife to the delivery room. Around here you'll never find a male over the age of three anywhere near a house where a woman lies in labor.

The Kilo believe that childbirth leaves a woman vulnerable to attack by spirits. As the child comes out, it leaves an opportunity for evil spirits to invade the woman in the absence of her child.

Weird, but also logical in a way.

Because of this belief, the men of the village want nothing to do with women in labor. Turning to leave, we retreat as quietly as we can, hoping not to be noticed. I don't think the woman with the water saw us, which is why Jeff stopped so short – he figured out what was going on as he turned the corner and didn't want to be spotted.

The sun is sinking and we start home. Standing between our houses a few minutes later, we decide to have dinner outside at our place. With only two families left on the job, you might think we would socialize every night. But like anywhere else, with anyone else, it depends on a lot of things: moods, energy levels, and whether or not we just want to be left alone. But tonight we've got a lot to talk about.

I leave to tell Rachael about our plans, while Jeff goes to do the same with Wendy. Twenty minutes later we're gathered around the picnic table in our back yard.

We talk over the day as we wait for the charcoal to ash over and be ready for cooking. The labor pains continue unabated with occasional screams carrying down the path.

Because of their superstition about women in labor being vulnerable to evil spirits, Kilo women generally suffer as quietly as they can. With the possibility of possession on her mind, she doesn't want to call any more attention to the birth of a baby than she has to.

"Wow – I've never heard anything like this before!" Rachael remarks as another cry goes up.

"I know," Wendy replies. "Something must be wrong."

"If it goes on any longer, they might come get us. Did you make a belly wrap for this one?"

The "belly wrap" is Rachael's invention to help ease the discomfort of pregnancy. Being pregnant does not reduce a woman's work load. She is still expected to tend the garden, care for the kids, and gather firewood, all with a swollen belly and an aching back. Rachael wanted to sew together something to help ease a woman's strain, and the result is "the belly wrap."

I don't understand what it is or how it works. I only know it's made of elastic lace (which I didn't even know existed), making it strong *and* comfortable. It works with the push-pull tension between a woman's back, shoulders, and belly.

The end result reminds me of an athletic supporter crossed with a sports bra and a pair of suspenders. Whatever it is, however it works, the belly wrap has become quite a hit.

At first the women weren't so sure. It took one particularly miserable woman to break down and give it a try before word could spread – the crazy thing actually worked! That was over a year ago and ever since Rachael has kept busy sewing them for each woman who gets pregnant.

"I did. It's Nengat – can you believe she's only sixteen?"

"Sixteen and pregnant," Wendy mutters. "What a crazy place."

"As if it's any different back home," Jeff says. "Last time we were back, I think that was actually the title of a TV show!"

"So what do you think of Henry's bright idea?" I ask, changing the subject.

"I don't know what to think," he replies. "On the one hand, I'll be glad for the help with the airstrip, that's for sure!"

"I know what you mean," I answer. "I was starting to worry that the men would be getting sick of machetes now that practically everybody has one."

Hacking back the jungle to keep the airstrip clear is a constant task. With abundant rainfall, tropical temperatures, and a year-long growing season, the jungle greedily reclaims any cleared land. A never ending source of amusement for me is hearing people bemoan the disappearing rainforest. Seriously, have they ever been to the jungle?

No one who has spent time in the jungle can say that with a straight face.

No doubt land is being cleared at unprecedented rates. Cattle farming and logging are both booming industries, and both require vast tracts of land. They tend to go hand-in-hand, actually. The loggers come through first and the ranchers bring herds to graze behind them.

The thing that never makes the news though, is that the jungle grows back almost as fast as it can be harvested.

There are over two million square miles of jungle – more than half the size of the United States. Imagine everything from the Pacific to the Mississippi completely covered in trees.

Would you be worried about running out of trees?

Yeah, me neither.

Only someone who has never flown over the jungle for hours and hours without seeing a single break in the triple canopy could think we're in danger of losing it.

I actually think of the jungle as a living thing – one gigantic organism. And when you cut out part of it to build an airstrip, it gets angry. And when it gets angry, it punishes you by re-growing everything you just cut out.

Jeff and I are in a constant battle against the jungle to keep the airstrip free of obstructions and overgrowth, but Henry's decision promises to make that a whole lot easier.

"But on the other hand," Jeff continues, "I don't like the idea of the mission work being associated with forced labor."

"I thought they could opt out. It isn't forced labor, is it?" Wendy asks.

"Okay, maybe not forced. Let's say 'coerced' instead."

"You're right," I put in, looking to Wendy. "Henry says any man who doesn't want to follow the new chief can 'opt out,' as you put it. He can take his family and move away."

"But still," Jeff says, "there's tremendous pressure to stay."

"Oh, I won't deny that," I reply. "I'm with you on the 'coerced' bit."

"I don't like it," Rachael interjects. "The whole thing seems wrong. Why would Henry do this?"

"He's trying to help, I guess." Even as I say it, I'm aware of how lame it sounds.

At this point the coals are ready. I put the chops on the grill and turn in time to see a woman rushing around the side of the house. She is out of breath and clearly excited.

We call her Jane because when we first came to the village, she was so painfully shy, it took more than a year to learn her name.

To the Kilo, a name is more than an identifier. It is a possession, and only the person "possessing" the name can give it out.

If they don't want to tell you their name, no one else will either.

And a person does not "say" their name. They loan it. If they tell you their name, they are loaning it to you. It is your responsibility to care for it, to not hurt it (by using it to insult them), and to guard it, in case they do not want to loan it to anyone else.

With no name to call her, we resorted to "Jane Doe." After she warmed up and decided we could be trusted with her name, it was too late. "Jane" stuck and we've called her that ever since. Another different thing about the Kilo attitude toward names is that because a name is a possession, only one person can have it. You'll never find two Kilo – dead or alive – with the same name.

Jane barrels around the corner, breathing hard, and so excited she can hardly talk. Seems to be a lot of that going around today!

"Woah – calm down." Rachael tries to talk to her, speaking softly in Kilo.

"*Noonta bawan!*" Her chest and shoulders heave with each breath.

Come quick!

With delayed recognition, it dawns on me that we haven't heard a cry from down the road in a while. That realization, plus Jane's hurried approach and obvious distress, leads to the easy conclusion that something is wrong.

"*Nengat!*" I cry. "Something's happened with the baby."

Jane doesn't speak English, but she gets that I'm talking about her friend in labor. She nods vigorously, beckoning Rachael to follow her.

"*Noonta bawan!*"

Her stress has reached a fever pitch. I'm afraid if we don't do something now, she'll just grab Rachael and drag her by the arm.

"You two go," I say to Rachael and Wendy. "We'll put out the fire and follow after."

"No," Rachael says. "No men, remember?"

Right. Jeff and I will have to sit this one out. Not that either of us would be much use in a delivery room. I can do a lot of things, but attend to a woman in labor? Yeah, right.

They bolt after Jane, grabbing a medical kit from the house as they do. Labor complications are not unusual here, and the girls have both become somewhat proficient as midwives.

The Kilo women may be superstitious about childbirth, but they're pragmatic enough to get help when they need it. This is not the first complicated birth the girls have attended to!

4

Two men can only say so much about childbirth, so we talk about other things.

The coals are hot and the food is ready to go. But the girls are gone. Nonetheless, we figure we might as well eat. We have no idea when the girls will be back, so I grill the meat and vegetables. We'll set theirs aside for later – hopefully sometime tonight.

We sit and eat, but we don't talk much. We're each lost in our own thoughts, and communication is limited to monosyllabic requests for condiments. This is the stuff that drives our wives crazy – the way we talk sometimes, or rather, don't talk.

We tell them it's just guy stuff, but they don't seem convinced. They're firm in their belief that if two people don't communicate in polite niceties, someone's feelings are going to be hurt.

I have explained that guys don't have feelings, but they just gave me a look that I knew better than to challenge.

I can't keep my mind off Henry. The collective grief of a village in mourning and the unprecedented nature of Henry's decision is a potent mix, and I can't help but dwell on it. The possibility of not having to devote so much time and energy into maintaining the airstrip is intriguing.

But I don't see how this move could be anything but a referendum on our work here. The majority of the Kilo are more than tolerant of our presence. With only a few exceptions we've had a warm welcome from just about everyone.

Ernie Bowman

Call me cynical if you want, but I have to think the machetes we bring with us and the medicine we give out might have a little something to do with that.

The question is though, are machetes and medicine enough to buy what is going to amount to a village-wide subsidy of the missionary work here? While almost everyone has been friendly, not everyone has been receptive to the teachings about *Kaale'*. We have always maintained that we are not here for our own good health. We have presented ourselves to the Kilo exactly as we have presented ourselves to supporting churches back home: international representatives sent by God to bring the good news about Jesus Christ to the Kilo people.

But religious tradition runs deep. We are, quite literally, attempting to overturn and correct many generations of animistic beliefs that the shamans have a significant personal stake in.

Besides the question of personal belief, these men gain social standing and profit from the practice of the traditional Kilo religion. When white men come to teach and preach something different…well, you'll have to forgive them if they don't line up and cheer.

Henry was unique in those early days. He was among the first to embrace "the new words." God caused Henry to be favorably disposed to us and our work.
Nothing else can explain his utter willingness to embrace the gospel message. Or for that matter, his intuitive grasp of English. After Henry, there were a few more early successes, but things plateaued after that.

Much of the village has taken a "wait-and-see" approach and are gauging our own commitment. If the message of *Kaale'* is indeed so very important as we claim, they will see if our actions bear that out. If we pack up and leave, the verdict will be clear. We are persevering and that has won us some respect, but not everyone is convinced yet. But neither have they rejected us.

Henry's choice may threaten that.

This all bounces around my mind as I sit at the table with Jeff. The sun is now well on its way to setting. I'm thinking about heading inside the screen tent before the mosquitos come out when the stillness is shattered for the second time tonight:

"*Noonta bawan!*"

I hear Jane before I see her, jerking my head toward the sound. Jeff is facing me across the table, his back to the house. He swivels so fast he's probably just got three splinters in the seat of his pants as Jane races around the corner shouting.

"*Noonta bawan!*"

If I didn't know that phrase before, I doubt I will ever forget it now. Rachael and Wendy have already gone – Jane has to be talking to us. For the life of me, I can't imagine why.

5

"Noonta bawan!"

She's screaming it now, having stopped at the corner of the house.

I look at Jeff. Jeff looks at me. We both look back at Jane, who has started to hop up and down like a child who needs the bathroom.

"Noonta bawan!"

Urgency is written all over her face and even though we have no idea what she wants, we jump up to go with her. I bang my knee on the tabletop as I climb off the bench.

Limping slightly, I see Jeff tumble to the ground. For the second time today, we can't keep our balance as we race to answer some unknown emergency. It's a good thing the girls aren't here to see this because we have got to be the worst rescue squad that God ever assembled!

I'm limping from the crack of my knee against the table. Jeff is scrambling to his feet, all arms and legs. Rather than wait, Jane is disappearing around the corner. I realize whatever is going down must be serious. Yup, I'm perceptive like that.

I can't believe a girl who just ran across the village twice in the span of a few minutes is outrunning us, but it's true. If it hadn't been for the fact that we stumbled onto the location of the screams earlier, we might have lost her.

Catching only fleeting glimpses of her back, we follow Jane to the house we had backed away from earlier.

There is no sound coming from anywhere and it's eerie – almost like the jungle itself has stopped growing to wait and watch to see what will happen. Jane is at the front of the door and I skid to a stop in front of her, almost losing my balance in the process. Captain Coordination strikes again.

"*Tibla,*" Jane says flatly.

You wait.

"What?!" I start to protest.

"We just ran all the way –" but she's turned on her heel and is gone.

Jeff limps up ten seconds after me, a pained expression on his face, sweat beading on his forehead.

"What happened to you?" I ask, looking him over.

"Twisted my ankle falling out of your picnic table," he pants, hands on knees again. "Feels like I sprained it."

"Nice one," I say dryly.

I am secretly (and probably sinfully) relieved that I'm not the clumsiest one on the team.

"You should be more careful."

"Maybe I should sue the homeowner."

"Yeah," I start to reply, not even trying to hide my sarcastic grin. "You do that. Let me know how it –"

I'm cut short by Rachael, who pulls back the door and pokes her head out:

"You guys gonna sit there and bust each other's chops or come in here and help us?"

"But Jane told us to –" I start to say, but again, she's gone. For the second time in under a minute I've been left talking to the air.

Not something I'd like to get used to, but at the moment we've got bigger problems. Jeff wipes the sweat out of his eyes and I'm surprised to see my hands are trembling. Ignoring it, I push through the curtain door and step over the threshold.

I've seen a lot during my time in the jungle. *Nothing* has prepared for me this.

6

The house is all one room, about fifteen feet square. Not square in any technical sense, just roughly the same length on all four sides. The cooking fire is off to the side, vented through the wall by a chimney.

My ADD kicks in and despite the absurdity of it all, I wonder how they keep the chimney from burning up. There's no sheet metal in the jungle and it appears to be made of bark. But bark would burn up if it were hung over the fire like that. I wonder if....

"Jeff!"

It's Rachael. She's used to my mental wanderings but is apparently not in the mood at the moment.

"Over here."

I look over, noting six other people crammed in the tiny space as my eyes travel. Rachael has made it across to where a woman is lying in a hammock, legs splayed out over the sides, baby belly bump protruding over the top. Wendy is standing next to Rachael, back turned to the room as she rinses a rag in a water gourd. I walk over and begin to speak:

"We came over as soon as we could. But I thought we weren't supposed to –"

"How many minutes do we have left?" she asks, cutting me off.

"Minutes? For what?"

"Internet. How many minutes do we have left on our month?"

"I don't know," I answer. "Maybe a third. Why?"

We pay for satellite internet from a company in the capital. It costs an arm and a leg, but the only alternative is short wave radio. It's tough to send a picture attachment by radio, so we pay up and purchase a few hours' worth of time each month.

"I need you to go home and do some research."

"You want me to what?"

"I think the baby is breech. She's been in labor for hours with no progress. I've got no idea what to do; but if we don't do something, I'm afraid we'll lose them both!"

Her words come out in a rush, but I follow what she's saying. Nothing gets an ADD head-case to focus quite like an urgent task. I spin on my heel, noting the clucks and the chirps of disapproval from the Kilo women as I do so. I start to say "Let's go!" to Jeff, but he's not behind me.

It's full on dusk outside but I'm still momentarily blinded as I step out of the dim house. Not like "middle-of-the-summer-and-you-just-walked-outside" blinded. More like, I-just-stood-up-too-fast-and-my-eyes-are-fuzzy-around-the-edges. I pause and feel the curtain flap against the back of my legs. It takes three seconds for my vision to return and when it does, Jeff is looking at me expectantly.

"Well? What gives?"

"Breech birth," I say, as if I've said it a hundred times instead of one. "Rachael's not sure what to do. She needs information and needs it fast."

I take off running as Jeff falls quickly behind, limping on his bum ankle. I consider stopping to let him catch up but decide to press on. He'll understand.

I take the steps two at a time and I'm inside with the laptop open on the table just seconds after that. We've called our internet service many things, but "fast" has never been one of them.

I don't know if this company has launched their own satellites or just pirated bandwidth from some second rate Russian job left over from the Cold War. Based on how fast this page is loading, I'm betting on the Russian thing.

The page finally loads and I enter a search term for "breech birth emergency" when Jeff pokes his head in the door.

"I'll fire up our computer too. If we search different sites we can cover twice as much ground."

"No – wait!" I say as he ducks back out. "Don't do it. If we both log on it'll clog the feed and make everything three times as slow."

I have no idea why this is a thing, but it is. If both of us are logged on to the internet at the same time, instead of just doubling the load time for webpages and documents, it nearly triples – we've timed it."

"Rachael has some medical books in the closet. Top shelf on the right. Start looking for Labor and Delivery."

I check the screen and start to scroll.

Images are clogging things up so I narrow the search parameters for text pages only.

That cuts the results in half, but now I've got to read to see if they'll be useful. Scanning page after page, it feels like this is taking forever. I click back for pictures and wait.

Jeff has three books piled on the table in front of him. He's got one flipped to the index, looking for any entry with the word "breech" in it.

"So what exactly is a breech birth anyway?" he asks, not looking up.

"It's where a woman goes into labor but the baby –"

"Never mind – got a visual here!" Jeff interrupts.

I swear, one day I'll get to finish a sentence.

"So you're telling me that kid is coming out backward?"

"That's what Rachael thinks."

"Then you probably want to take a look at this."

The book is called *A General Guide to Home Nursing*.

I remember when we bought it.

Rachael was garage sale shopping for last minute things we would probably never need (Does anyone actually *need* anything they buy at a garage sale?) when we came across the house of a doctor who was recently retired and moving to Florida.

In the process of cleaning house he was selling books and medical manuals.

Rachael had picked this one and a few others, insisting they would "come in handy." I wasn't convinced; but for garage sale prices, I couldn't pass up the chance to make my wife happy.

Right now those books were looking like the best purchase I'd made. Laid out on the page in front of me are a series of images depicting various forms of labor and delivery distress – including a breech birth.

I don't know how old this book is, but I can't imagine that the science of delivering babies at home has changed much since then.

God bless garage sales!

Grabbing the book, I pull it toward me as I abandon the computer, sliding over one chair so Jeff and I can look simultaneously.

None of these pictures look good for any woman or baby experiencing what they depict, but they all have detailed explanations on what to do when they happen.

"We've got to get this to Rachael!" I jump to my feet, banging my knee on the underside of a table for the second time today.

"You go. I don't think I can run anymore," Jeff says with a wince, looking down at his ankle.

Even with his shoe on I can see his ankle is badly swollen.

"There are ice packs in the med kit and ibuprofen in the medicine cabinet," I say over my shoulder as I head for the door. "And see if you can find anything else in those other books."

I leave Jeff at the table, his ankle swelled up and his lap full of old textbooks. For at least the three thousandth time this year, I thank the Lord for my wife. It might have been sheer luck, but this book might just save someone's life. Two – if she can save the baby.

I run back and start to duck inside before pausing to knock – which is a dumb thing to do because the door is a curtain and curtains are pretty difficult to knock on. I pause long enough for Wendy to appear beside me.

"Nothing online, but I found this in the closet," I say, handing her the book. It's open to the right page and she looks it over as I pass it into her hands.

"I was dumping the dirty water when you came around the corner. I'll take this and see if it helps. At this point it certainly can't hurt."

Her face is grim and has lost its usual shine.

"I've never seen a delivery like this one, Ian. She's been in labor for hours with no progress – none."

"Any idea what's wrong?"

"Other than breech birth? No. But we're starting to doubt even that."

"Oh?" I ask, not sure what she means.

"We've seen breech births before. This doesn't feel like that. Nengat is really suffering – it's like somebody has pushed pause on the whole thing."

Having nothing else to contribute to the cause or the conversation, I turn to head back. I stop and look back when Wendy speaks again.

"Ian?"

"Yeah?"

"You and Jeff better start praying. I think it's all we've got left."

"Did we ever have anything else?"

She doesn't answer, and I don't expect her to. I start the walk, distracted and wondering how this will end up. I pass the spot where Jeff and I collided and it makes me remember his injured ankle.

I can't do anything to help Nengat, but I can tape an ankle.

I pick up the pace and head for home.

7

I left in such a hurry that the door is standing ajar and I can see Jeff in a chair at the table, his ankle propped up on a throw pillow from the couch.

Throw pillows, I think to myself.

If there ever was a distinctively feminine home accessory, it's got to be throw pillows. Even in the jungle we have more throw pillows in our house than there are uses for them, mostly – if you ask me – because throw pillows have no uses. This, of course, ignores the obvious fact that Jeff is currently putting two of them to good use as he cushions and elevates his ankle.

Chasing away my hypocritical thoughts, I close the door and head to the hall closet where we keep extra medical supplies. As I do, I catch a glimpse of the laptop open on the table.

Great, I think to myself. *The internet's been up the whole time I've been gone. Whatever minutes we had left will be gone now.*

Instead of turning to the bathroom, I go to the table, silently grousing about internet fees and the loan sharks that we buy time from. Ever the picture of missionary joy and tenderness, I'm about to ask Jeff why he didn't close out the browsing window when my eyes land on the screen.

The last page I loaded but never looked at is displaying a list of search results. The third headline down the list catches my attention:

"Breech Birth Complications and What to Do About Them"

Forgetting our dwindling internet time for the moment, I click the link and ask Jeff, "Did you see this?"

"See what?"

I notice as I turn that his eyes are closed, and it registers that he hasn't moved since I walked in the door.

"This search result," I say, indicating the screen that is loading line-by-line.

"Sorry man, I didn't see a thing. After you left I got the ice and stuff for my ankle. I figured there was nothing *I* could do, humanly speaking, so I've been sitting here praying about the whole thing. I hate that prayer is my last resort, but it's better late than never, right?"

"Yeah. Right." I say absently, as text appears on the screen.

You'd think a couple of missionaries would be more spiritual than that, but I guess spiritual independence is a hard thing to get over…even for missionaries.

"Take a look at this," I say, pointing at the laptop. "It's a list of complications for breech births – specifically written for at-home deliveries."

"Looks like a forum for midwives – didn't even know there was such a thing."

The text has fully loaded and I can read all the headlines as I scroll down the page.
There are images for each one, but those have yet to come through.

Jeff reads out loud as I scroll through:

"Frank Breech. Complete Breech. Cord Entanglement. Chin Lock. Footling Breech....these mean nothing, Ian. We don't even know what we're looking at."

"I know, I know. We need those images if any of this is going to make any sense."

"Slow internet," Jeff says with sarcastic amusement. "Who would have thought we'd have First World problems in a Stone Age jungle?"

Normally I'd have a response to a crack like that but an image just appeared on screen. I don't know how and I don't know why, but something in cyber space cut loose and the images appeared on the screen, almost simultaneously, like a digital avalanche.

"Now we're cooking with peanut oil," I say, in my best Phil Robertson voice.

Jeff isn't impressed with my impression so I give it a rest and scroll to the top of the page, unplugging the cord and checking the battery life as I do. The display says sixty percent – should be enough. I stand up quickly, but this time I'm careful about my knee.

"Where are you going?" Jeff asks.

"This does us no good at all," I reply over my shoulder. "But it might be of some use to the girls. I'm taking it over."

By now I'm out the door but not so far away yet that I can't hear Jeff call out:

"Hey – disconnect! You'll waste the minutes!"

Right.

Using one hand to try and maneuver the cursor and the other to hold the laptop, I do my best to sever the internet connection as I walk.

It's not working, and in my fumbling I almost drop the computer.

"Hands like an amputee, Allen," I mutter.

I pause on the path long enough to verify the page is fully loaded before I disconnect from the satellite. Tucking the computer under my arm, I start jogging.

Outside the house where Nengat is in labor, I pray that we're not too late. Remembering the curtain, I knock on the wood post that serves for a door frame and call out to Rachael. She slips out and sits down next to me.

"How's it going in there?" I ask for the second time today.

"Dark," she replies, indicating the sky.

The sun has set. Dusk is gone and we are fully into night at this point. In the absence of other lights, the little orange bulb that indicates "power on" for the computer seems extraordinarily bright.

"What's with the computer?" Rachael asks.

"Jeff and I found something online that might help. I don't know if it's any use or not, but we figure you'd better take a look."

I open the laptop and punch in our password.

We don't have kids around the house and there is a zero percent chance the Kilo will attempt to log onto our computer, so it's not like we *need* a password.

But I can't figure out how to disable the built in feature, so it stays. I'm sure there is an online help forum, but when internet minutes are limited and expensive, it doesn't seem like that big of a deal.

"Take a look at this," I say, handing Rachael the computer.

She takes it from me with an exhausted sigh. Scrolling through the page, she mumbles half-sentences, evaluating options as she goes.

"Frank Breech...no.....Flexed Breech? Maybe. But if it was...no, can't be. Wouldn't be able to move, and this little guy has gone down and come up already...."

She lapses into silence as she looks. *How does she know it's "a little guy?"* I wonder. It's probably just an expression but I never get the chance to ask.

"THAT'S IT!" she yelps. I practically jump off the ground. A small animal actually skitters away to our right, just like in some cheap movie.

"It HAS to be that." Her voice has quieted slightly, but is still firmly in the "outdoor voice" category of decibels.

"Has to be what?"

"Chin lock. It's got to be chin lock. But that would mean..." her words trail off as her mind chases an idea.

"It says here that a possible complication of twin birth is that the babies might get turned toward each other, one breech, and the other normal. During birth, their chins may become interlocked like puzzle pieces, preventing normal movement into the birth canal."

"Twins? She's having twins?"

"There's no other explanation; it has to be that."

She goes back to reading, her eyes frantically scanning side-to-side. Her mumbling commentary is back, but it makes little sense to me.

"Most common in young mothers...first pregnancy....that all fits. Breech/vertex....inverted fetuses...Great – C-section recommended."

"You're going to do a C-section?"

"No way – I'm not that nuts!" Rachael says as her face whips up from the screen. There's an unexpected little grin there that seems totally out of place to me.

"But your horror is a bit odd coming from the only one of us who has done jungle surgery!"

"Yeah, but I..." I protest, before thinking better of it and conceding her point. "Touché'."

"No, I am not doing a C-section. We have no drugs. No pain killers. No sterile environment." She goes back to reading.

"According to this," she says a half-minute later, "the first twin can be manipulated back up into the uterus with a Zavanelli maneuver. It has directions! Ian, if we can get that first kid to move off the other one, we can get him born before it's too late!"

I truly have no idea what is happening, what any of this means, or why my wife is so excited about the possibility of performing a labor and delivery "maneuver" she isn't familiar with.

But I also haven't assisted in the delayed birth of multiple problem pregnancies. She has.

Shaking my head, I take the computer and help her to her feet. Giving it back in case they need to reference the site again, I give her a quick kiss on the cheek."

"Good luck. I haven't the foggiest clue what you're talking about, but we'll be praying."

"Thanks Ian!" She says with a smile that just about kills me.

Nothing in the world makes me happier than seeing her excited about something. Through the doorway she goes – back to work. Stunningly, I have heard nothing from inside the house since I sat down.

But as I turn to walk away, I hear Rachael's pitched voice explaining things to Wendy. I don't wait until I'm home. I pray as I walk. I am marveling again at the mess and the adventures that come out of nowhere in the life of a jungle missionary.

I have no doubt there would be a whole line of lawyers, hospital administrators, bureaucrats, and assorted official types of people back home who would cluck their tongues in disapproval if they were here. But here we are again, facing down a complicated medical problem in a do or die situation.

And right now a law suit or a legal policy book would be more out of place than a jungle missionary turned labor and delivery nurse. Walking home with a confidence I shouldn't feel, I take all of this and lay it at God's feet.

Like I told Wendy earlier – we don't have another option.

8

I'm in the recliner dozing when footsteps on the porch wake me up. Jeff went home hours ago. I just can't sleep in the bed when Rachael is gone, so I'm camped out in the living room. The door cracks open as I drop the foot rest on the chair, squinting across the room with blurry eyes.

Rachael pokes her head in the door and looks around tentatively. I stand up and my knee reminds me of my earlier clumsiness.

"Hey – you're back!" I exclaim, starting across the room and hiding my limp as I go.

I take two steps and stop. Rachael hasn't come into the house; she's still on the porch, holding a blanketed bundle.

"What are you doing?" I ask. "Get in here, I've been worried about you."

"I can't," she whispers.

"What do you mean you can't?" I ask, reaching for her arm to pull her inside.

"I mean, I can't. And keep your voice down. You'll wake her up."

"Wake her up?" I ask, not lowering my voice at all yet. "Who are you –"

"Shh!" Rachael hisses.

She takes a step back from the door, motioning me out with her hand.

I step forward and close the door softly, noting the first streaks of gray coloring the sky behind her.

I'm wondering several things at once: Why is my wife holding a baby? Why can she not come inside?

"They were twins – chin locked, just like I thought. We were able to move the one off to the side and deliver them both. I'm afraid we may have damaged her shoulder though," she says, indicating the child in her arms."

"Wow, that's great!" I say, still wondering exactly what is going on. "So what's the deal, I mean, why can't the kid come inside? And why do you have Nengat's baby?"

"They were twins," she's looking at me like I'm supposed to know what that means.

"And…"

"And that's bad. She can't come inside because of the spirits, apparently."

"I'm sorry Rachael. I'm not following."

"I'm not sure I understand it all either, but I'll tell you what I know. Just keep your voice down."

"Okay, but why do you have her?"

"They were going to kill her," she says flatly, her eyes flashing with anger.

"Kill her!?" I practically shout. "Why?"

"Shh!"

Her shushing is almost as loud, but I wisely decide not to point that out.

Appropriately shushed, I clamp my mouth shut and wait for her to continue.

She talks for almost ten minutes without stopping. At first I break in to ask questions, but it's clear she doesn't know anything other than what she's telling me. From Rachael I learn for the first time about Kilo superstitions and beliefs about twin babies.

As she explains what she learned from the other ladies in the house, I am both horrified and mystified.

The Kilo believe in what my seminary professors would have called the preexistence of the soul. It's the belief that all the souls of all the people ever to be born exist in the spiritual world.

At the time of conception, a pre-existing soul is joined to the newly created body of the child. Where the Kilo belief veers from what I learned in college, is that they believe each mother is only capable of hosting one soul at a time while she is pregnant.

This means that in the case of twins, one of them doesn't have a soul.

The tribe believes the twin born first is the one with the soul. With twin births in the tribe the second baby doesn't usually survive.

We have seen that happen before and always chalked it up to the fact that the second twin took longer to be born and that somehow contributed to its death.

Not the Kilo.

They believe the second twin dies because a body cannot live without a soul.

In the cases in which the second baby does not die, the Kilo believe it is because the baby has been possessed by evil spirits. They already believe the spirits are waiting to attack the mother through the birth process, so I guess it makes sense.

Rachael was able to discern from the other women that they assume this is what happened to Nengat and her twins.

She was loud throughout the birth process, repeatedly crying out in pain. Looking at things now I can understand why: complications of chin locked twins can't be exactly comfortable.

The Kilo women see things differently. They think that by crying out so loudly she alerted the evil spirits, who took advantage of her labor and attempted to possess her.

"Fortunately" for her, she was carrying twins. Because of this the evil spirit ended up inhabiting the body of the second twin. This explains why the child was born alive, and also why Nengat was able to survive the "possession" attempt.

I say it was "fortunate" for her only because it isn't a fortunate situation for the second baby. The women all assume the child is possessed by an evil spirit and want nothing to do with it.

Including Nengat.

After the twins were born the first one was given to Nengat, and the second one was set aside.

Literally.

They put the baby off to the side and they left it.

No one cared for it.

No one washed it off.

No one wanted to touch it. Rachael tried to care for the baby but they physically prevented her.

Because no one wanted to be in the house with an evil spirit baby, they forced everyone out and just left the baby there by itself.

Even Nengat, having only minutes before delivered twin babies after a long and complicated labor process, was taken out of her own house.

"She just left her baby there?" I barely manage to keep my voice down.

"Everyone did. They forced me out of the house and insisted that I leave."

"But you didn't leave."

It was a statement, not a question.

"No way," she says defiantly. "There was no way I was going to leave that baby alone in that house to die."

"What did you do?"

"I acted like I was leaving but as soon as I turned the corner I doubled back through the jungle. I crept along, keeping my steps light so I didn't make any noise. I worked my way through the trees back to the village path her house is on. When I could see her doorway through the leaves I waited."

"You just sat in the jungle? By yourself? In the dark?"

There are a few things you learn pretty quickly around here, the first of which is:

Never go into the jungle after dark by yourself.

"What choice did I have?" she asked. "I wasn't going to let this kid die!"

"How long were you there?" I am amazed at both her bravery and her foolishness.

"Not long. I waited maybe five minutes before crossing the trail. I maybe should have waited longer but I couldn't stand hearing her cries anymore."

"So you just walked in and took the baby?"

"Basically, yeah," She says with a shrug.

"I dashed across, slipped inside, and picked her up. I calmed her down and she eventually stopped crying. Poor thing has to be starving but I don't have any way of feeding her. I just rocked her until she fell asleep, exhausted. When I was sure she was asleep I slipped out of the house and came here."

"Wow." That doesn't even begin to cover everything she just said, but it's all I can say at this point. "Why can't we take her inside?"

"They think she has an evil spirit. When her crying stops they'll think she died. In the morning they'll go in but she won't be there. It won't take long to figure out where she's gone to. They'll come looking for her."

"Right," I say, still not getting it. "But why can't we just take her inside? It's not like they'll barge in and take her back, especially if they think she has an evil spirit."

"Any house with an evil spirit has to be torn down. It's unclean. If we take her inside they'll want to burn down our house."

"But what are we supposed to do then?" I can see why it might be a bad idea to bring the baby inside, but I don't see what other option we have.

"I don't know. But I couldn't walk away and let her die."

She looks down and there are tears in her eyes. I have no idea what to do. What I know is that, like my wife, I won't stand around and let the baby die.

My mind is swimming with questions and I can't stop imagining the pitfalls we've just stumbled into.

Right now though, all I can focus on is the child sleeping in my wife's arms. A flood of emotion overtakes me as I look at the two of them, and I'm surprised by the hot tears in my own eyes.

We had tried for years before being told that we would never have kids of our own.

People tried to tell us it was "part of God's plan," because life on the mission field would be "so much easier without kids."

Whatever.

They might have been right; but it still hurt to hear it and I've fought the bitterness for years.

Looking at my wife holding a newborn baby is a sight I never thought I would see.

I know it's an irrational thought, but I can't help hoping we can keep her.

We could raise her.

We could love her.

We could give her a home.

We can't do nothing and let her die, so why not adopt her as our own?

I reach out to take Rachael in my arms, the closeness of our hug impeded by the baby between us. Neither of us seem to mind; and as we stand there all together for a moment, I close my eyes and let my mind dream.

The baby squirms and Rachael pulls back.

"Here, hold her for a bit. I'll see what I can come up with."

Before I know what's happening, I'm holding the tiniest human I have ever seen and I'm terrified I'll break her.

Rachael disappears into the house while I turn to look out over the front rail of the porch, feeling this baby girl squirm in the crook of my arm. I'm not naturally a touchy-feely person and I avoid holding other people's kids whenever I can. But this is different. Something about this just feels right.

Somehow, it also feels ominous.

9

Raising my eyes, I allow them a moment to adjust to the middle distance past the porch. When they do, I just about jump out of my skin – Henry is standing at the bottom of my steps! I have no idea how long he's been looking up at me.

"Henry!" I say too loudly, setting off another round of whimpers from the baby. "What are you doing here?"

"Not me. What are *you* doing?" he answers, clearing wondering why I have a Kilo baby in my arms and not another Kilo anywhere in sight.

"It's Nengat's. Or, at least she was."

"I know. I have been told."

There is no emotion or trace of warmth in his voice at all. Other than moving his lips to speak, he hasn't twitched a muscle. The expression on his face is one of blank exhaustion.

"What do you mean you 'have been told'?" I ask, immediately on guard. Henry's demeanor is off. Normally he's joyful, smiling, and energetic. Right now he looks empty, sullen, and expressionless.

"If you keep the child, you will have to leave."

"What?!" It's more of a statement than a question and it comes out involuntarily.

Henry makes no effort to reply.

He still hasn't moved.

His eyes are pointed toward my face, but they aren't focused on anything at all.

I've read that soldiers in war can develop a "thousand yard stare."

I wonder if that's what I'm looking at right now. While his words hit home, Rachael comes back onto the porch.

"Here," she says, holding up a disposable plastic bag full of milk. "Maybe this will work."

Henry looks off to the side, his gaze still not focused on anything. I glance between the two of them. She picks up the tension of the moment.

"Is everything okay?" she asks softly, reaching for the baby.

"I don't know," I answer so that only she can hear.

I hand the baby to Rachael; and as I step off the porch, I see her drift over to the chairs on the other end. Henry turns to walk around the back of the house. He doesn't say anything, but I know I'm supposed to follow.

The five second walk to the back yard feels like five minutes. My brain is working overtime to make sense of what is happening. The questions all spin together:

What does he mean we'll have to leave?

How did he know to come here?

Where has he been all day?

What has he been doing?

Have the other men come back from the jungle yet?

As Henry stops and turns to face me, I can't keep quiet any longer:

"Henry, what are you talking about? Why do we have to leave?" I know, real subtle, right?

"The baby," he says, as if that explains everything.

"What? Come on, you've got to give me more than that!"

"The baby has an evil spirit. It cannot stay. As tribal leader it is my duty to make certain it does not."

"Evil spirit?! Henry, you know that's not true!"

Henry may not be a Bible scholar, but he is not spiritually ignorant either. At this point he knows what the Bible teaches about the soul of a person.

"You are correct; I know." His reply is soft, with none of the edge that was there just a second ago. "But the others do not know these things yet. They still believe the old ways."

"If you know, then why don't you explain it to them? Call a meeting of the elders, get the people together, and teach them!"

"It is not so easy."

"Tell me what I'm missing then. Help me out here! Why is this complicated? We're talking about a baby!"

Henry's sigh is heavy, like an exhausted man who can't go on but has resigned himself to the fact that he must.

His empty eyes turn away to look over my shoulder. His gaze is fixed on something at the back wall of my house.

More likely it is fixed on nothing.

He is silent. I swat at bugs, growing impatient. Normally I'm pretty good at waiting in silence, but after three minutes with nothing more from Henry, I'm about at my limit.

My impatience is about to get the best of me when Henry takes another deep breath and begins to speak. At first he is so quiet I can barely hear him.

"There is much that you do not know about Kilo death," he begins, then immediately pauses again. The silence that follows is not as long as the one I just endured, but it is more profound somehow. Ten seconds in it is broken by the soft cry of a newborn baby, coming from the front of the house.

"You are right when you say that I know different. But I am right when I say I am the only one. My people do not accept the word of *Kaale'*. For me to convince them that the child does not have an evil spirit would be impossible."

He tells me of the Kilo beliefs about evil spirits and childbirth. Most of what he says I have already heard once tonight from Rachael, but somehow it feels wrong to tell him that. I just let him talk.

He is much more certain of himself in telling the details than Rachael was, even including some parts she didn't know. When he is done I am glad I didn't interrupt.

"So you see, my people will not be convinced. Even the word of the chief will not be enough to convert their minds, to say nothing of their hearts."

"Okay – I can see how you're right about that. But what will happen to the baby?"

"So long as the child lives, the people believe the evil spirit will not leave."

He says nothing after that.

I look up at his face, thinking that surely he cannot mean what I think he means!

But his eyes are expressionless. Empty. He looks as if his body is inhabited but his spirit is dead. There is no life in his features, only exhaustion and a look of hollow resignation.

"Wait...that means...but you...?" Captain Articulation is clearly on the job tonight. "You can't possibly mean..."

"It is the only way."

I'm shocked. No, that's not right. I feel no shocks because at this moment I feel nothing. My legs are numb. My head feels like a bowling ball. I stumble back unsteadily onto the picnic table. Placing my head in my hands I try to process what I've heard.

Surely Henry, my friend, our first convert and indispensable partner in the mission work, did not just say what I am certain I heard him say.

The numbness goes away only to be replaced by a profound ache.

I am aching for the little girl. I am aching for my wife. I am aching for myself. I am aching for Henry. He cannot be serious, can he?

Looking up, I see his expressionless features in a new light. His face is not the face of a man exhausted from work and stress.

It is the face of a man who has steeled his spirit against the assaults of his conscience. He has to know that what he is saying is not right, but he is apparently determined to see it though.

"You think me a sinner," he whispers. "You are right. But it is better for one child to die than for an entire family to be driven out."

I am almost too stunned to speak.

"What are you saying? You cannot be serious – she's just a baby!"

His eyes remain fixed over my shoulder, refusing to look at me. I know I shouldn't, but I throw any pretense of patience to the side. I'm yelling at this point and I don't even care.

"Listen to yourself, Henry! I know you! You know this isn't right! What you are doing is *not right!*"

If this were a movie, the echoes of my voice would sound dramatically around us as we faced off in a great moral confrontation for the ages. But this is not a movie. And nothing echoes in the jungle. Sound is just absorbed by the trees around us.

There is no echo. There is no dramatic moment. The insects don't even stop their nighttime chorus – the world continues spinning as if nothing is happening. It's just the two of us in the back yard, not looking at each other.

We sit there in stillness, the silence hanging heavy between us. Henry's gaze is still unfocused and any patience I had for this day is long gone. I know he is devastated, and I know I should wait him out. I know I should be patient. But I can't. I can't take his remote expression. It is distant. Impersonal. He is using the distance of his stare to separate himself from the reality of what he is proposing. I'm yelling again:

"Look at me! Henry! *Look. At. Me.* You cannot. Just kill. A baby!"

At my outburst, his eyes immediately sharpen and his gaze bores into mine. As we stare at each other across the ten feet of back yard space that suddenly feels like ten miles, I finally see it.

The pain.

His eyes are brimming with pain.

"There is much that you do not know about Kilo death." His eyes are locked on mine, but his voice sounds far away and hollow.

"Then tell me," I whisper. "Tell me, Henry."

And he does.

He speaks without pause, which is unusual enough. What is more unusual is that his eyes never leave mine. It is so unlike him, so unlike the Kilo way, that I am fully taken aback.

Several times I am almost overwhelmed by the urge to break off the stare, to look away. But I don't. I look at my friend. I listen.

Henry tells me about his day: of his grand plan to make the airstrip his privilege garden, of how this is not a popular decision, of how there is grumbling and complaining among the men.

His father would never have done such a thing, and the people know it.

As he says these things, I am reminded that Henry is a man who lost his father to death, just the day before. He did not ask for this. He did not ask for the pressure of being chief. He did not ask for the immediate crisis of Nengat's twin babies.

Henry tells me of the subtle resistance he has been feeling because of his friendship with me. He is not universally trusted in the village. Choosing the airstrip as his privilege garden compounded that problem. He acknowledges that maybe it wasn't the best choice; but what's done is done, and he cannot change it now.

He tells me of the men who came immediately to work with him that day. Shortly after I left him at the airstrip that morning, they pledged their loyalty to him as chief and joined the work on his "privilege garden."

As the day went by, more men had come, but it was never the steady flood that had begun the day.

By ones and twos they came to him, but it was the ones who had not that made the biggest impression.

According to Henry, they will not peaceably accept him as chief. If it were only one or two, the expected next action would be that they simply did not rejoin the others at all. It is rare – but not unheard of in Kilo history – for a man to go his own way when a new village leader is chosen.

It is also rare – but again not unheard of – for the rest of the men in the village to take so long returning to pledge their loyalty to the new leader.

The way Henry sees it, the men still in the jungle aren't exactly sitting under trees and twiddling their thumbs by themselves.

They're talking.

To each other.

About him.

And the fact that many of the men who did come back from the jungle took their sweet 'ole time doing so, is further proof that Henry is on thin ice as the village leader right now.

He doesn't use that expression of course – the Kilo know nothing about ice – but it's the distinct impression I am left with. His place is perilous and precarious.

Henry is afraid that his friendship with me and his endorsement of our work has tainted his tenure as chief already.

He's worried that the men in the jungle are plotting a coup.

He's worried that many of the men on his side aren't as firmly on his side as it might seem. If they were genuinely excited to have him as village leader they would not have waited so long to come back from the jungle. Their delay was meant as a sign. It isn't one Henry has missed.

The worst case scenario is that the men in the jungle come back to the village in protest. The men not firmly on Henry's side might then jump at the chance to join them, and a fight would break out to settle the issue.

This has happened before, Henry says, but not in his lifetime.

Henry doesn't want to fight, and he doesn't want to kill anyone – especially a baby that he knows for a fact is not possessed by an evil spirit.

As chief, it is Henry's responsibility to ensure that the "evil spirit" in the baby cannot stay at the village. The way to make that happen is to kill the baby which will release the spirit. If he doesn't kill the baby, the rest of the village may revolt with the men in the jungle.

If all of that happens, the best that Henry can expect is to be forced out of the village with the baby. Exile to the jungle isn't *necessarily* a death sentence, but it's close. Worst case is they all get killed in the uproar and the baby dies anyway.

"Wow," I say, ever quick with the helpful comments.

"Now you know. Now you know why the child cannot stay and why you, if you keep her, cannot stay. It is not permitted."

"But," I protest, ever the rational American. "You're the leader. I get that it won't be easy, but they have to listen to you. Don't they?"

"A leader leads only if others follow."

His cryptic reply is so very close to the American ideal that I am momentarily distracted and taken back to school in my mind. It sounds a lot like the "consent of the governed" clause in the Declaration of Independence. Recalling this bit of history is interesting, but not exactly relevant at the moment.

"Yeah, I get that. But there has to be another way. You can't kill a baby."

"What other way?"

"I don't know, Henry. I really don't. But I know God wouldn't want it. And when God allows a hard thing or a test, he always leaves a way out. There is a way. We just don't see it yet."

"Look harder, my friend. I must act soon."

Without another word, he turns and leaves, walking away to leave me sitting there, too stunned to move and too exhausted to think.

10

The rest of the night goes by, but it feels like a week. It is now after noon the next day but I haven't left the house yet. Rachael hasn't left the porch. After Henry disappeared, I sat in the back yard for an hour before stumbling inside.

There has been no movement in the village, not even the usual trek out to the gardens at sunrise. Everyone is staying inside, and the place still feels like a ghost town. If it weren't for the smell of cooking fires and the rising smoke drifting off over the jungle, I would have thought the village was abandoned. It certainly *feels* abandoned. I'm going crazy with worry, racking my brain looking for a way out of this thing. So far I have come up with exactly nothing.

Well, not exactly nothing, just nothing workable. The best I've come up with is to call for the mission plane, take Rachael and the baby, and leave for the capitol. This has the upside of saving the baby's life and preserving Henry's leadership as chief, but the distinct downside of abandoning the work.

The track record is clear - if a missionary pulls out, the hope of re-gaining a tribe's trust is just this side of zero. Tribes always identify the actions of a missionary with the character of their God. If I leave the work, they will conclude that Kaale' has also left them. It isn't fair, but life rarely is.

A living example of that fact is currently sitting on my porch.

Rachael has been there since yesterday, holding that baby.

Miraculously the baby has taken milk from the baggie. I guess when you're hungry anything will do. We'll run out of baggies eventually, but that's a problem for Future Ian to deal with.

Just before we left for the field, one of the couples at our church had a baby that wouldn't nurse, so they called in a lactation consultant to help. No one would ever confuse me for a lactation consultant, but I have to wonder what one would say about our methods here today. Probably nothing good.

The downside of our little arrangement has been the effect of cow's milk on the baby's digestion. Or at least I think the milk is to blame. Let's just say that diapers during the night have not been pretty, especially for a couple of people who have no diapers and no diaper wipes.

Rachael has been making do with old t-shirts for diapers, but at some point we'll need a better solution. Future Ian is going to be busy.

The sun is up and the last of the mist is burning off the jungle. It looks like a postcard. Birds are swooping. Monkeys are calling. If someone saw me standing in the back yard staring just now, they might say I look "transfixed." Maybe I am, but it's not the jungle that holds my attention. I am transfixed by a lack of good options.

In other words – I'm stuck.

If I hand the baby over to the village, she dies.

If I don't hand her over, there will likely be a riot and Henry might die.

Along with me.

And then the baby.

If I take the baby and leave, the work stops and we have wasted years of our lives in this place. The Kilo never have another chance to hear the gospel and Henry still might not last as chief.

I'm praying silently when I begin to hear muffled sounds of life. Nothing distinct, just the occasional thump or murmur that indicates people are moving about.

Cocking my head to the side I stop to listen, straining to hear.

The noise is coming from the village and I head that way. As I walk around the side of the house, the baby cries again. It's a tiny sound – almost inconsequential – and the jungle swallows it immediately, as if the world itself wants to extinguish her.

I turn the corner to the front of the house and Rachael is standing at the edge of the porch, craning her neck to look down the lane.

When she wouldn't come inside I rigged up some mosquito netting to enclose the half of the porch where she spent the night.

At the moment she has her nose pressed up against it, neck craned as she struggles to get a view of whatever is happening just out of sight.

"What do you see?" I ask, climbing up the steps, but stopping just short of the actual porch itself.

She is looking down the lane, but I'm looking at her. I've never been the sappy type; but seeing her standing there holding that baby, I am hit with the weight of everything at once.

Our childlessness, the possibility of losing the work we put in here, the possibility of losing Henry, and the possibility of losing this baby girl.

I don't even know her and already I am attached in ways that words can't describe.

Intellectually, I know I can't possibly have a deep love for someone I don't know. But there is something there – longing to protect and a desire to keep her safe.

I'm angry and tender all at once. It's a confusing mix that scares me and thrills me at the same time. I feel my cheeks flush, and I'm glad Rachael isn't looking at me.

"I think they're avoiding us," she says. "I keep getting glimpses of people moving in the tree line."

"Avoiding us? Or avoiding her?" I ask, indicating the baby.

"Probably both but I don't know why –" she stops in mid-sentence, having turned toward me."

"Ian, are you all right? Are you crying?"

"No," I say, entirely too quickly, turning my face away from her. "It's just something is making my eyes burn." It's a lame response and I know it. Even as I am saying the words, I don't know why I'm doing it. It isn't like I have anything to hide from my wife.

"Well if your eyes ever stop 'burning,'" she says with enough playful inflection to let me know she doesn't believe me, "you might want to find out what's going on."

"That's where I was headed," I say, grateful for the change of subject. Jeff and Wendy come out of their hthere ouse as I start down the lane.

"You see what's happening?" Jeff asks.

"Not really," I reply. "Rachael thinks she can see people moving in the trees, but that's it."

"There's a gathering in the Commons" Wendy says. "We've been watching people walk through the jungle across the back of our yard all morning. It's weird."

"I'm heading down to check it out. Maybe you can stay with Rachael?"

I don't want to leave Rachael by herself right now. At first Wendy hesitates, clearly wanting to see what's happening in the village, but something stops her. Maybe it's the look on my face. Maybe it's the leftover effect of my eyes "burning" from just a moment ago. Whatever it is, she agrees and heads to our house while Jeff and I start down the path.

"How many people?" I ask as we walk, side by side, as only white men will do in the jungle.

"I don't know. It's hard to tell because they've been keeping inside the tree line. Maybe a few dozen.

"Any idea what's up?"

"None. But I get the distinct impression they're avoiding us. Or that girl. What was Rachael thinking?"

"She was thinking we couldn't just let a baby die!" I say, with too much force.

"Hey man, I didn't mean anything by it. It's just I – "

"I know, I know," I say, cutting him off mid-protest. "I didn't mean to snap at you. I'm just frazzled, you know?"

"Yeah, I get it," he says, dropping the subject.

We walk in silence but don't go far.

It takes only a few minutes to cover the distance to the curve in the path. It winds around to where the village proper begins. Despite the hodge-podge look of things, a Kilo village is actually a strictly organized thing. The houses are set in a rough set of concentric semi-circles, with the Commons as the central hub.

The outer ring of houses are for younger warriors with minimal stature in the tribe. As we pass the first few, the stillness is almost palpable. Most don't even have smoke rising from fires.

There are rough paths between houses and between rings of houses; and as we move closer in, we start to see movement. There are a few stray children around and an occasional thump from inside a couple of huts. The sounds of wood being split into kindling is soft, but distinct.

The last ring of houses is always reserved for the oldest men with the most stature. There is a constant slow motion shift of who lives where. It happens throughout the year as older men die and younger men gain prominence in the tribe. I can't tell you exactly how it works, but I know that the houses we are passing now are for the most prominent in the tribe. Passing the last house, we come to the Commons.

There is a meeting house on one end and an open square on the other. The meeting house is full of people. But a second look reveals that they are all women and children. The men are across the square. They are lined up and facing each other.

The meeting house is an open sided pavilion similar to one that would be found in a park. Half walls support posts that hold up a thatched roof.

The women and children crowded into it will be the favorites of the men who are arrayed in the open square.

Each Kilo man has a favorite wife, usually his first or his most fertile. Her children will be the ones he loves best. The sounds we'd heard coming from the huts that we passed on the walk here were from the other wives.

The children we saw roaming the paths were the children of those less favored wives.

It is an honor to be chosen as the wife of a prominent man – even his second or third.

None of this makes any sense to me, especially the part about how a man will consider it more honorable for his daughter to be chosen as the third wife of a tribal elder, rather than the first wife of a more junior man.

This boggles my mind because second and third wives are more likely to be beaten than a man's first. Their children are likely to be fed only after the children of the favorite wife, and the second or third wives are always given the more unpleasant work to do.

With a shake of my head, I pull myself back to reality. Now is not the time to parse out the marriage differences between cultures. One glance at the open square is enough tell me much bigger problems are afoot.

The meeting house is packed, but the open square is only a third full. There are two lines of men standing shoulder-to-shoulder, facing each other in what amounts to a rough oval, open at the ends.

Picture an empty set of parentheses and you've got the basic idea.

I gape and take it all in. I realize I am staring. Jeff notices too and his elbow jabs my ribs as he talks out of the side of his mouth:

"Ian – close your mouth," he whispers

Another man steps from the tree line and joins the line of men closest to us.

There are twenty guys in his line but only twelve in the other. The line with fewer men has spread out and they take up as much linear space as the larger group.

The effect is to preserve the shape of the lines in parentheses form, but with more space between men.

"This is it," Jeff whispers.

Right away I know what he's referring to. Every tribal cultural is distinct – to a point.

They each have different adaptations of what to eat, how to build a house, or how many wives a man might take; but there are similarities too.

One of those similarities is what we might call civil war.

Normal disagreements are handled one-on-one, with men squaring off playground style. The fight follows a familiar pattern, and the loser typically drops in rank within the tribe.

Occasionally the loss is bad enough that he has to move out of a more prestigious house and into a less renowned area of the village. But other missionaries have told us their accounts of what happens when a disagreement spills over and encompasses the entire tribe.

What Jeff and I are looking at seems to be exactly that. Every man holds a weapon. Some have huge clubs, while others have chosen smaller, almost bat-like sticks. No one is unarmed.

Jeff and I stand immobile. We have no experience with any of this, but we've been told enough to know it's not good.

Someone always dies.

Often multiple people.

What is at stake is not only control over the tribe but personal survival as well.

When an issue this serious divides the tribe, everyone chooses sides to fight it out. The losers are forced to accept the total dominance of the winners, vacating any huts of the inner ring they may occupy and moving, at the very least, to the outer rings of the village.

Plunder is not uncommon, with the victors forcing the defeated to leave their possessions and provisions in the hut as they leave.

This means the loser is not only humiliated, but must begin the process of building a home and a life all over again.

The meeting house is jammed.

The women don't relish the thought of watching the conflict play out, but they know that anything left in the home of the men who lose today will be subject to seizure – including them.

It's not common but it has been reported that some men retain those women and children for themselves. The fear of that happening today has led to the crowd we see right now.

"What do we do?" I hiss.

"Nothing – that's what."

"But they'll kill each other."

"If we intervene they'll kill us too."

Every part of me is screaming to do something. There will be blood today, but Jeff is right and I know it. This is one of those excruciating moments of missionary life when non-intervention is the right thing. I can only make it worse.

Nothing in my training has prepared me for this. I search my memory but nothing in the Bible seems to touch on tribal civil war. I'm begging God for wisdom but the words and advice of my adolescence seem like a cruel joke at this point: *What Would Jesus Do?*

I can't even begin to guess.

We've been standing here a bare two minutes, but already three more men have emerged from the jungle. No one has said a word, but everyone moves as if by instinct.

After joining a line, the new men stand like statues.

A stare down conveys courage the world around.

The battle will not be won by intimidation but they attempt it nonetheless. The climactic standoff from *The Good, the Bad, and the Ugly* comes to mind, along with the weigh-in stunt before every heavyweight boxing match.

But the revolvers in the movies are loaded with blanks and the media know the boxers won't throw a punch at weigh-in. Today holds no such guarantees.

This is not a movie.

There are no media and no referee.

The tension is as high as the jungle canopy.

Violence is in the air.

By silent agreement, we edge over to the nearest building. We don't want to leave, but we also don't want to intrude. We creep along until our backs are against the wall.

Our movement precipitates something in the square. A final man emerges from the forest and takes his place with the smaller group. When he does, both sides take a step back in unison. No cue was given, but the men move as one.

Two heartbeats go by.

Then three more.

Ten seconds of silence feels like an hour.

A man from the larger group breaks off. He is a third of the way down the line and he takes two steps forward before freezing in place again.

The threat is clear – *Step up if you're man enough* – but no one does.

Two heartbeats go by. Then three more. Ten seconds of silence feels like another hour.

A man from the smaller group steps forward, mimicking the first man.

Each line closes ranks to eliminate the gap created by their combatant, and I realize what is happening. These two will fight first.

Ironically, for a guy who hated English class, I picture the confrontation in terms of living punctuation.

The empty parenthesis from before has been filled by a colon (:) until the men begin to move.

With measured movements that border on pageantry, they each turn to face the other and take one exaggerated step forward. They are ten feet apart – close enough to be a threat but not yet within striking distance.

I recognize them both.

The man from the smaller group is Mentab, a middle aged Kilo man with middle stature in the tribe.

His home is located on a path halfway to the front. He has a wife and two sons but has never seemed fond of them. I have always thought he seemed unsatisfied and unsure of his place.

I guess a middling stature in any community will do that to a man.

The man facing off against him barely qualifies for the title. Nabtal is one of the youngest men in the tribe. He has a wife but no children. Rachael told me last week that she thought the woman was pregnant. "She's glowing," Rachael said.

Newly pregnant American women smile all the time, but the Kilo are much more sanguine about these things.

The birth of a child is always welcome, but with food scarce and manual labor a fact of life, miscarriages are frequent. Because of this fact the pregnancy smiles come out significantly less often for Kilo women.

I pointed out to Rachael that I hadn't seen any difference in how often or how wide Nabtal's wife has been smiling lately, but she paid me no mind.

"Doesn't matter," she said. "She's hiding it well, and I'll bet there isn't a man in the village who knows. Maybe not even Nabtal. But a woman knows."

And sure enough, as I paid more attention over the next two days I saw a difference. Not in her – I still can't see any glow – but in the other women. It wasn't anything I would have noticed before, just subtle glances and small helps that confirmed things – at least for Rachael. *I* still don't see any glow.

All of that flashes through my mind as I watch Nabtal square off against Mentab.

Without warning, Mentab's arm swings out. His club is large – almost unwieldy. Wide on the end with a tapered handle, it is reminiscent of a child's red plastic bat. But this is no game, and he's not swinging at a whiffle ball. Winding up, he aims to strike Nabtal upside the head.

But faster than Mentab can react, Nabtal is in motion. Instead of backing away from the blow, he lunges forward. Invading the space between the two men, he is now inside the arc of Mentab's strike.

He'll get hit, but it will be a glancing blow.

Without breaking his forward motion, Nabtal jabs upward with his own weapon.

It's more like a billy club than an oversized baseball bat. In other circumstances he would have been out gunned. But in this case, the lighter weapon works to his advantage. With Nabtal jabbing from the hip and Mentab swinging from the shoulder, their blows land simultaneously. Mentab's strike glances off of Nabtal's shoulder.

It will bruise but it's not a serious injury. Mentab, on the other hand, takes the blow full force in the chest. The smack of weapons on flesh and the wet **crack** of a rib snapping are unmistakable.

I'm not a pacifist, and I've been in my fair share of fights. But even still, I cringe at the sound of the blows. None of the men in the square flinch or blink an eye.

Mentab is momentarily paralyzed but Nabtal isn't done. Momentum carries his elbow up and over Mentab's head. There is a split second pause as his arm reaches the peak of its swing before crashing back down. The butt of his club crushes Mentab's head, who immediately collapses to the ground.

If this were a video game or a movie, Nabtal would finish him off with a killing stroke. Instead, Nabtal stands stock still, staring down down at the crumpled man beneath him.

The exchange is over almost as soon as it started. My brain has barely recognized what happened and I struggle to process coherent thoughts. Nebtal stares down at the older man for only a moment.

Then, with unnatural calmness, he takes a step backward. Laying one arm across his belly, he balances an elbow on a forearm, his chin resting in the palm of the hand. It is a twisted parody of the "Thinker" statue but the club in his hand and Mentab's body lying in the dirt ensure that no one mistakes this for a philosophy discussion.

At length, Mentab begins to stir. Only when he regains consciousness and attempts to stand does Nabtal stir from his pose. As he rejoins the line on his side of the square I notice for the first time that all of the men have adopted the same Thinker-like pose. The stare down continues as Mentab struggles to his feet, bleeding freely from his head.

No one helps him as he staggers back to his place. Impossibly, he assumes the same pose and acts for all the world like he didn't just almost die. He is staring straight ahead, but even from this distance I can see that his eyes are unfocused. He has a concussion at least. A fractured skull is more likely. And yet he doesn't move. No one moves. Even the birds have gone still.

In the heavy air of late morning the only thing moving is the blood running down the side of Mentab's face. I desperately want to do something. Anything. I know I can't help. I don't even know what "help" would look like right now. I don't know who the good guys are. I don't know who the bad guys are. I start to say something to Jeff, but I'm cut off by movement in the square.

"Do you think that –"

Two more men step out from their lines. First one and then the other. They repeat the sequence of moves from Mentab and Nabtal. Everything about the exaggerated sequence is the same and soon enough they have squared off in the middle.

Once again, there is a young man of little stature facing an older man with prestige. The older man again caries a hefty club, while the younger man grips something more wieldy. The stare down commences, followed by a strike.

The older man rears back to swing his club and the younger man darts forward with a thrust. I've seen this movie before, and it ends the same. A glancing blow to the back and a stunning strike to the chest. But this time it ends differently.

The younger man is knocked to the ground by the force of the club, while the older man only stumbles back a step or two.

Clearly he was more ready to accept the jab; and just as clearly, the younger man did not expect so much force from the club.

But with one man on the ground, they retreat to their lines. The damage inflicted by Nabtal was far worse, and I don't understand why these two quit after one exchange of blows. Clearly they are still capable of more.

I glance at Jeff. His eyes are wide and his nostrils are flared. His breathing is labored and I can see tense muscles standing out in his forearms.

"What's up with that?" I ask, assuming he will be thinking what I'm thinking.

"I don't know. Any idea what they're fighting about?"

"No. I've never seen anything like this."

"I don't see Palal or Henry."

Henry.

Glancing around I note that he is not present, which is highly unusual. The chief – disputed or not – should be at any communal gathering of the tribe.

He doesn't preside like a judge but if things were to get out of hand, it would be his word and the force of his position that would bring them back under control.

But he's *not* here. Neither is Palal. Palal is a Kilo non-conformist. He does his own thing, which is rare enough in the jungle. Palal makes a point to be contrary about everything.

Tribal life is community minded, to the point that the chief is often more like a Prime Minister who builds consensus than a king who rules by decree.

If the tribe wants to send a delegation across the mountain to make contact with another village, Palal will declare the idea to be foolish.

If the chief issues a particular order, Palal makes a show of doing the opposite.

This is not normal Kilo behavior, but it has never been a big deal because he's harmless, and mostly alone. He keeps to himself, and the only people who take him seriously are his wife and brother. Occasionally he'll manage to pull in a supporter or two, but never very many.

Every church I've been a part of has their own Palal. They usually deal with him the same way: by occasionally indulging, but mostly ignoring him.

A sinking feeling in my gut says that this wasn't such a good strategy. Their absence feels wrong. Palal is the malcontent-in-residence and Henry is the yet-to-be-confirmed chief. Their absences cannot be a coincidence.

During my exchange with Jeff, two more men have stepped forward. They move carefully in unison and we are truly in the dark here. There has never been a missionary report that mentioned this. This is the third round and I am starting to get a feel for the sequence of events. Unfortunately they remain the same.

The men step forward.

They turn, close the distance, wait, a first strike, and a counter strike.

The only thing different is that the man who strikes first doesn't go for the head. Jentabe is an older warrior but not an old man. He is old enough to be experienced, but not old enough to be an elder. Apparently he has seen enough of this fight to form a new strategy.

He strikes a downward blow aimed at the shoulder of Benal, the younger man opposing him. He's trying to incapacitate the club arm.

But with movements so quick they turn his arm to a blur, Benal flicks the club upward to block the initial assault. The weapons clash in the air with a sharp break – like a baseball bat on a fastball. After blocking Jentabe's initial swing, Benal jumps back half a step – his weapon is broken.

Benal needs a new piece of lumber.

He won't be getting one.

Sensing his advantage, Jentabe presses the attack. He steps and swings, working his club like a lumberjack with an axe.

Benal may have lost his weapon, but he hasn't lost his speed. He has never seen a dime, but he just stopped on one. Dropping into a crouch, he turns his body to the side and faces ninety degrees away from Jentabe.

The kinetic energy generated by his body would have surely been enough to send him toppling over if he hadn't immediately transferred it to his arm.

Benal's roundhouse swing moves into the path of the onrushing Jentabe. The change of angle and his sheer forward momentum give Jentabe no time to react.

Benal's broken stick catches Jentabe across the shins as his arm sweeps through its arc. Benal's weapon lodges between his legs like a stick in bicycle spokes. The resulting effect is the same.

Jentabe immediately crashes to the ground, his body tripping over Benal's crouched form. With the unexpected fall and the added obstacle of Benal hunched in front of him, Jentabe is unable to get his arms out and he pitches forward to the ground.

His nose hits first and breaks on contact. The dirt of the open square is unforgiving, compacted from years of use.

His shoulder hits next as he rolls while Benal twists without rising to his feet. Jentabe rolls once and comes to rest ten feet from where he fell.

Only then does Benal rise from his crouch.

With his chest rising and falling rapidly, he stands and stares until Jentabe begins to stand as well. Only when both men have risen to their full height does either make a move to his line.

Benal is missing his weapon, having left it broken where it fell, but Jentabe has taken the worst of things.

A baseball sized knot has already risen on his shin, and he holds one arm tightly to his chest.

His nose is broken and bleeding profusely.

The club he retains hold of is the only bright spot he can claim.

The three confrontations have resulted in two serious injuries. The kid gloves are off and the men are playing for keeps.

I am stunned and paralyzed.

Fights in the village normally involve only a handful of men: the primary adversaries and a backup or two. Never has the violence escalated to this level. If this continues, men will die – many of them.

I stand helpless as a child, wondering if the village can survive this, not only the fighting itself, but its aftermath as well.

Even if they all survive, I cannot imagine their living in peace after brutality like this.

The fourth pair steps forward, and the expressions on the faces of the others have yet to change.

At this point the pattern is clear: almost all of the men on the one side are younger. Almost all of the men on the other side are older.

As I survey the two lines I can identify exceptions: but for the most part we are looking at the world's most literal generation gap. But this generation gap has not been established by clothes and cemented by music. It is being established by animosity and cemented by blood.

I do not know this fourth pair well. I know their names, but that is all. Even still, I am already wincing in anticipation when I feel an impact in my own ribs. Not a smack, but more of a nudge.

Jeff jabs me and as I look he juts his chin towards the sky. I follow the path of his gaze, and what I see could be a Weather Channel advertisement. Dark clouds swarm and roil, churning bigger from the inside out.

Just as quickly as my eyes jumped to the sky, they focus back down.

While I was looking at the clouds, the fourth pair went through the pre-fight routine. Fat rain drops fall sporadically as the final stare down continues. Children whimper, nervous about the weather.

Over the course of my life I have lived in Michigan, Iowa, and Indiana; and in every place the people all said the same thing: *"If you don't like the weather, just wait five minutes!"* It's a lame joke that gets told way too often, probably because there is some truth to it, especially in Iowa.

But even out there on the plains, the weather had never changed this fast.

Three minutes ago the sun was out and the sky was clear. Now the sun is gone and an artificial twilight descends.

A heavy blanket of humidity hangs in the air. The drops of rain come faster – more than a sprinkle but less than a shower. My eyes flit between the sky, the men, and the pavilion.

The sky is an unnatural shade of black. The men haven't moved. The pavilion stirs slightly. Packing in tight to avoid the rain, the women have crowded together away from the open sides.

The sprinkle has become a downpour and I squint through the rain. The fourth pair are gone – I must have looked to the pavilion long enough to miss it. I manage to make out the new combatants and I see the biggest mismatch yet.

Pulan is Palal's brother and the oldest member of the tribe. With no official records and no birthdays, no one is certain who is actually the oldest; it's more of educated guess than anything else.

But no one can remember back further than Pulan, which makes him the *de facto* oldest.

Unlike the customs in some tribes, being the oldest doesn't mean being in charge here. However, just like everywhere else, being old does mean being slow.

Pulan does nothing in a hurry, which might explain why this fifth confrontation has already taken more time to get to the actual fighting than all the others combined.

Standing opposite Pulan is the youngest recognized man in the tribe.

Calea has only recently taken a wife.

He has no children and he has no standing.

He is the Kilo equivalent of a kid who graduates high school and turns eighteen the next day.

He's an adult, but just barely.

I can't make out Pulan's face but it wouldn't matter if I could. He may be old and slow, but he is brave and experienced. To show fear would be a sign of weakness. No doubt his face is a stoic mask. I am equally certain that Calea is nervous, but the rain is now lashing the square in sheets so I can't see him clearly.

There is no wind – only the rain. It falls heavily enough that the men appear as indistinct human shapes. Calea strikes first.

He attempts to copy Nebtal's thrusting jab; but in his youth, he lacks ferocity. Pulan easily blocks Calea's attempt but, at his age he is unable to counter effectively and they resume their stalemate.

I loved thunderstorms as a kid. I would sit on the back porch and watch the rain. We would start counting as soon as we saw lightning, waiting for the thunder to follow. The sooner the thunder came after the lightning, the closer the storm was.

The bolt of lightning is blinding. It's the world's brightest camera flash followed immediately – almost simultaneously – by a crashing roll of thunder. The sound is terrible and awesome, as if the sky itself were being torn.

The light fades and I see Calea make a fateful mistake. Startled and distracted by the thunder, he flinches. His shoulders duck and his head swivels involuntarily towards the sky. He realizes his error almost immediately, but it is too late.

Pulan never lost focus and when Calea flinched, his club was moving. Dragging his old arm through the rain as hard as he can, he makes it through most of the swing before Calea catches up and looks back down. There is nothing he can do but to jerk his neck in a futile attempt to evade the blow.

Against a younger man, Calea would have certainly lost his life, maybe even his head. Against Pulan, the blow catches him on the ear, sending him sprawling. The momentum of the swing carries Pulan into a stumble of two steps before he can stop himself.

Calea lies prone.

Pulan stands facing him.

The rain is unabated

Over the rushing of blood in my ears I hear a small sound. The low groan begins slowly and culminates in a sharp crack.

Not the crack of whip, it is the amplified crack of breaking wood that I can feel in my chest like bass at a concert. The first crack is followed by three others in immediate succession, which allows me to orient my ears to the sound. My head jerks up and I inhale sharply, choking on the rain that comes with it.

The tallest tree in sight is scorched and smoking. As I watch, it begins to fall. About a third of the way down the trunk is split. Half remains upright; half detaches, foot-by-foot. Initially the tree is moving in slow motion. I watch as it separates and falls away.

The rain does nothing to dampen the sound as a series of rifle-like cracks punctuate the air. The slow motion lasts for only a second. As the top third of the tree separates, it falls open with increasing speed.

Mesmerized by what I'm seeing, I stand frozen and watch.

It isn't until the entire thing has broken off and the tree is moving at full speed that I actually realize what is happening. The trunk is not falling into the jungle – it is falling into the square!

My brain registers this but as quickly as I can think, it is over. There is no time to shout a warning. It wouldn't be heard if I could. The entire sequence takes only seconds and my brain can't form words before the ground vibrates under my feet.

The tremor is brief, but unmistakable. The tree hits with a thump that is quieter than I would have imagined. Only then do I realize that the impossible has happened. The main body of the tree, a full five feet in diameter, has landed directly between the lines of men. No one has been hit.

When you narrowly avoid a car wreck, you never start to shake until it's over. Perversely, it isn't until the danger has passed that your body reacts to it, which is exactly what happens here.

The rain beat incessantly, and for a fraction of time nothing else happened. But then – just like after a car wreck – the stress of the danger hit everyone at once.

In an instant, chaos ensues. Pulan jumps with an agility that belies his age. Several men break into a run, heading into the jungle.

Others shout and brandish weapons.

Still others are shouting at the men who are shouting at them, but pointing their weapons toward the sky. One or two have fallen to their knees, with one man lying prone on the ground.

My language skills are getting better, but they are not good enough for this. Between the rain, the shouts, and the tumult of the moment, I understand almost nothing that is said.

The little I pick out tells me that most of the shouting is about who is at fault for the tree falling. No one knows what happened, but they all seem certain that it was the other party's fault.

How anyone on the ground can be blamed for a tree falling in the jungle, I have no idea. I can only imagine what spiritual forces they think might have been at work. Whatever the reason, it doesn't last long.

Another bolt of lightning hits the square, followed immediately by thunder that doesn't roll or rumble – it explodes. The effect of the twin blasts is enough to silence the arguments and end the shouting.

Men scatter in every direction. Women and children from the pavilion do the same. Shouting. Running. More pointing. Screaming children. Pandemonium reigns. The noise rises and falls as people stream every which way.

That's not a cliché – there are people running in all directions.

I see a child left alone. He can't be more than three years old, and he is standing at the near corner, closest to us. His mouth is open in terror but his cries are lost in the noise of the rain.

The look on his face snaps me out of a daze and I run toward him. Before I have taken more than a few steps however, the boy is scooped up by a young woman; and they disappear down a path. Someone is pulling on my arm and I turn to see Jeff. He shouts over the storm:

"Let's go!"

Without waiting for an answer, he turns and runs down the path, opposite the direction we had entered the square. The hardened path sheds much of the rain, but already it looks more like a mud track than anything else.

The mud sticks to my shoes as we run. We dash through the village, catching sight of people as they duck into their homes. We make our way past the last row and onto the final stretch of trail that will take us to "our neighborhood." It is not an accident that our houses ended up where they did.

Even though we came here with their permission, the Kilo were hesitant about our presence here.

Specifically, they were worried that our missionary efforts were a front for evil spirits. Because of this fact, they insisted that we build our houses outside the village itself.

The shaman of the tribe had claimed that he could not protect the village against our spirits, and the people agreed that we must not build in the village proper.

Over time many of the people have grown comfortable enough with our presence that they will come *to* our house, but never *inside*.

That may change over time but so far it hasn't. They will stand outside and even come to the porch, but no one has been brave enough to venture inside. Regardless, the result was that Jeff and I built our neighborhood outside the village, a jungle suburb, if you can believe that.

Jeff and I stumble up to the porch and under cover for the first time since the rain began. We are both soaked to the skin and then some. The water streams off us and pools at our feet before seeping between the boards.

We stand in stunned silence, unsure what to say or think.

The silence is broken by Wendy, who is still on the porch with Rachael and the baby.

"What was all of that?"

"I don't know," I reply, giving the only honest answer I can.

"What do you mean you don't know?" Wendy shoots back.

"We heard nothing after you left for, like, twenty minutes. And then out of nowhere it started pouring and we heard gunshots and then a whole bunch of shouting!"

"Yeah, I know," I say. "But I don't know what it all means."

"And there were no gun shots," Jeff adds.

"Then what did we hear?"

"A tree falling but not just any tree," I say. "It was the Wapa tree."

"What?!" Rachael gasps from the other side of the porch. "They chopped it down?"

"It was hit by lightning," Jeff says. "It almost crushed a bunch of guys when it fell. Just missed them."

We fill in the girls as best we can but it takes longer to tell than it did to experience.

Wendy is uneasy when we describe the fighting, but Rachael is unmoved. When we get to the part about the rain, the lightning, and the tree, she shakes her head.

"It can't be a coincidence."

"What can't?" I ask

"The lightning and the tree – it can't be a coincidence that lightning finally dropped the Wapa tree, especially with what was happening between the people."

The Wapa Tree is a source of great superstition and reverence in the tribe. The Kilo legend is that a near mythical animal called the Wapa gave this land to the Kilo ancestors long ago.

The legend states that the Kilo and the Wapa were adversaries, not necessarily enemies but two groups competing for limited supplies of food and land.

The story goes on to say that the leader of the Wapa grew tired of the conflict. In order to end it the Wapa ceded the land to the Kilo, who tell of how the Wapa moved to a new land in the far north.

The exact spot where this agreement supposedly took place is – you guessed it – the very spot where the massive tree grew up: the Wapa tree.

It is easily the biggest tree around, or at least it was.

The legend may be based in fact or not, but there is no disputing the fact that there is an animal they call the Wapa. As to the actual history between it and the Kilo? Who knows.

"Wait," I say to Rachael, more forcefully than I intended. "Are you saying that the fight in the village caused the Wapa tree to fall? That doesn't make any sense."

"Why not?" Wendy interjects. "If what you're telling us is true, the village was on the verge of civil war. You know they wouldn't have stopped until the last man was standing."

"The way I see it," Rachael says, nodding in agreement, "God sent the storm to break up the fight. When that didn't work, he dropped that tree right into the middle of it all. The men scattered, the war was over, and the village survives."

"For now at least," Jeff mutters.

"I don't know," I say, "that sounds far-fetched to me."

"Everything sounds far-fetched to you," Rachael replies, her voice rising. "This isn't seminary, Ian. Not everything is going to fit into a neat case study from a text book."

"I know, I know," I say, trying to calm her down a bit. "I'm not saying it's impossible, just that I'm not sure that's what happened today."

"Does anybody have a better explanation?" Wendy asks, looking at Jeff.

Jeff is saved from having to answer by a sharp hist from the bottom of the porch.

"*Psst!*"

Not unlike a similar hist back home, it is the universal Kilo call for attention.

"Henry!" Jeff practically shouts. "Where have you been?"

Instead of answering, Henry walks up onto the porch. His steps are measured, almost mechanical.

"The Wapa tree fell," I say as Henry reaches the top.

"I know," he says. "I saw."

"Why is this happen–" I start to ask. But I choke on the words when I realize what Henry said. "What do you mean you saw?"

"I remained in the jungle. With Palal."

"You want to explain that?" Rachael asks. "Because we have no idea what's happening."

Henry looks to her and then pointedly to the baby she holds in her arms.

He is quiet and turns to the side of the porch.

He speaks firmly but with no malice at all.

"It is the child," he begins. "She has an evil spirit, or so they believe. I have managed to convince many that she does not have to die – but not enough. There are still too many who cling to the old ways, too many who would kill her."

Some of what he tells us we already know – about twins and evil spirits. But he also has many things to say that we have not heard before.

He speaks of ancient traditions for dividing the tribe when a matter of life and death cannot be decided by other means.

He tells how the men will align themselves with one side or the other, and then physically form lines in the open ground of the square.

The leader of each side must not be present. They must remove themselves from the village and not fight for themselves – that burden is borne by the men who align with them.

"But why do they have to fight?" Rachael asks. "And what are they fighting about?"

"They are fighting about her," Henry says, inclining his head toward the baby in Rachael's arms. "We are fighting about you."

"Me?" she asks, not understanding. "But why?"

"Because you have her."

Henry continues his explanation; and by the time he is done, I think I understand most of what has happened.

"What you're saying then," I try to summarize, "is that too many of the people still believe the baby has to be killed. Because of this, Palal convinced a bunch of them that Rachael is endangering the village by keeping her here and not 'releasing' the spirit," I conclude, using their euphemism for killing the baby.

Henry nods and continues: "Yes, but that is not all. Palal has many plans."

"Plans for what?" Wendy asks, her patience wearing thin with Henry's answers.

"Plans for himself. For the village," Henry answers, apparently oblivious to Wendy's irritation.

"But why were the men split up by age?" Jeff asks.

"Minds that have traveled the same paths for so long do not easily take to new paths."

And just like that, I get it.

"What Henry is telling us," I say, trying to shorten the communication process and hopefully head off the growing frustration. "Is that Palal is making a move on Henry.

"He is leading a coup, using the baby as an excuse to make himself the chief."

"I do not understand 'making a move,'" Henry says, "but yes, Palal wishes to be chief. He wishes to rule the village. He has many plans."

"Plans for what?" Jeff asks.

"Plans for you." Henry indicates with his hand that he means to include all four of us in that assessment. He is speaking *to* Jeff, but *about* all of us.

If this was a cartoon, a lightbulb would have just gone *ding* over our heads.

We finally grasp that Palal has seized on the twin opportunities of indecision over a new chief and Rachel's rescue of the baby. He not only aims to be chief, he wants to expel the missionaries! At first I can't believe it. After all, Palal has always been an outsider, even within the tribe, and has always seemed content with that.

At the same time though, it makes sense. Everyone has an ego, even eccentric loners. It is possible that his eccentricity and withdrawn nature have been a shield to his wounded pride at not being accepted.

Apparently, Palal sees our little missionary mess as his golden opportunity.

He can elevate himself to chief by eliminating the only real potential rival. At the same time, he can get rid of what he undoubtedly sees as an intrusion: the missionaries.

"Will he....*kill us?*" I ask.

"Be killed or leave," Henry replies. "What does it matter? You will be gone, and the Word of Kaale' will leave with you. My people will live in darkness, for none will believe what I say about him. I will not be here to say anything at all. There can be only one chief."

And in his eyes I see the truth. We may suffer banishment, but Palal would never take that chance with Henry.

If Palal succeeds, Henry will die.

11

Every hour I don't sleep that night feels like five.

The rain continues and the more thunder I hear, the more plausible Rachel's idea seems.

I had originally rejected the idea out of hand. I have seen too many radical claims get debunked way too easily.

I have grown weary of Christians who alternately blame or credit God for every natural disaster. I'm a cynical person by nature so that doesn't always help matters either.

The idea that God would send a specific lightning bolt to a specific tree in a specific jungle village during a specific tribal confrontation was initially just too much for me to accept. I have seen too many "faith healers" who turned out to be quacks. I have grown weary and wary of people who speak of summoning specific divine intervention on command.

My natural cynicism and a few literal presumptions about how things work sometimes make me closeminded about supernatural things, which is weird for a missionary; but it makes perfect sense in my head.

What does not make perfect sense however, is this storm. The jungle has seasons, just like every place outside of Hawaii. A major rain storm lasting for days or more is not necessarily unusual.

But a major rainstorm at this time of year most certainly is.

There are showers here year-round, but at this time of year they are always that: showers, not storms.

As the night wore on even I had to admit that something about this storm is different.

The morning breaks with a different shade of grey, but no proper dawn.

Henry left our porch last night almost immediately after our conversation about Palal ended.

Jeff and Wendy stayed long enough to talk and pray with us, but eventually they too trudged off through the rain. If their night was as sleepless as ours, I can only imagine how they're feeling.

Rachael and I spent the night on the porch. Until we know exactly what will happen, she doesn't want to risk the extra offense of taking the baby inside. At this point I am not sure how we could create any more offense than we have, but I wasn't going to argue with her.

With everything that we had learned and the violence of the day before, I wasn't comfortable leaving her out by herself. We made do the best that we could, but it was still a long night.

My back is one big knot, and I hurt all over.

I am sore from trying to sleep on a porch.

My head is killing me, my brain needs caffeine.

I look over at Rachael dozing on the make-shift bed we set up. The Kilo baby is mercifully sleeping in a dresser drawer next to her.

The drawer is padded with towels and Rachael has bundled her up as best she could, trying to simulate a Kilo mother in her hammock.

I am just about to go inside for coffee when I see Jeff step out onto their porch.

I decide my headache will have to wait.

Slipping quietly from our porch, I meet Jeff on his side of the lane.

"Hey," I say by way of greeting. To which Jeff replies with equal articulation:

"Hey."

"You sleep?"

"Not much. You?"

"Barely."

This monosyllabic interaction routinely perplexes our wives. They can't fathom why two people who like each other would communicate in such unrefined ways. That – and the fact that we don't ever hug – has always confounded them.

As perplexing as they find it though, it is Jeff's comfort level with silence and the fact that he has never tried to hug me that makes our friendship work.

I don't trust a man who never stops talking.

And I especially don't trust a man who constantly needs to be hugging everyone around him.

"See anything yet?" he asks.

"Nothing. You?"

"Nothing."

"How's Wendy?"

"Prayed out. Rachael?"

"Finally sleeping. The kid too, but we're running out of milk."

"We have a couple gallons in the freezer if you need them. How much do you have left?"

"She doesn't eat much; but even still we're down to maybe a day's worth."

"Okay. Hold on – let me go pull out what we have. Then let's take a walk and see if anything's happening."

He turns to go back inside as a thought strikes me.

"Jeff, hold up," I say. I'm not really thinking about what I'm saying, and it pops out before my brain can tell my mouth to shut up. "Maybe just pull out one. You know, just in case."

"Just in case wha-" he starts to say, but then gets it.

And in that moment I feel like a supreme jerk. My instinctual reaction was to pull out only one gallon of milk "just in case" the baby doesn't make it through this alive. Apparently my unconscious self doesn't want to take the chance of wasting a gallon of milk if the baby dies today. Milk is expensive and hard to get here, but even still, this is a step too far even for me.

"Nothing," I say, trying to recover. "Forget about it."

Jeff seems to understand what just happened in my head.

He looks at me for a second, but then turns back to the door. Two minutes later he's back outside and we turn to head up the path without saying a word. We walk the first thirty yards in silence before Jeff speaks:

"I pulled 'em both."

"Good. And thanks."

We pass the rest of the walk in silence, lost in our own thoughts. My mind is a swirling mass of guilt, confusion, and anger.

Standing out above the rest though, is the guilt.

I am crushed by the thought that Rachael and I have brought this bloodshed to the tribe. It was Rachael's decision to rescue the baby and my decision to shelter her that have put us in this position.

Images from yesterday flood my mind – the blows, the staggering and bleeding men, and the bodies lying in the dirt.

The guilt is a physical pressure on my chest. I have read about people who feel paralyzed by emotion, but until this moment I have never understood the reality of what they were describing.

My arms feel unnaturally heavy. I can actually feel my heart. And although I am walking freely, it seems as though my feet are dragging weights with every step.

Jeff and I have walked this route to the village hundreds of times over the last years. This time feels different. The jungle now seems threatening instead of intriguing. I know the huts teem with watching eyes.

The Kilo always watch us; it's just part of life. Every missionary is a novelty. There have always been watchers. There will always be watchers. But today their eyes feel menacing, not friendly.

Is it all in my head?

Maybe.

But perception has a nasty way of becoming reality, even in the jungle. The rain has let up some; but it is still a steady drizzle, and that isn't helping my mood or my mental attitude.

We make the turn into the open square and stop short. Looking at what is spread out ahead of us feels like deja vu all over again.

There are two lines of men spaced evenly apart, only this time they are on the near side of the square, not the far side. The pavilion is crowded with women and children. The Wapa tree lies unmoved where it crashed to earth.

Two more men emerge from the jungle, each coming from opposite sides of the square. They assume places on opposing ends of the formation, equidistant from the center.

Two beats of silence follow as the jungle itself seems to hold its breath. The unnatural stillness is broken as the men retreat one step each in a sudden move that smacks of coordination. The nearest man is now close enough for me to see the rainwater run down his back in a small but continual rivulet. If Rachael is right and God really did knock down their sacred tree to get the Kilos collective attention, it doesn't seem to have worked.

The weight on my chest has intensified and I'm short of breath. The tension is unbearable, and I legitimately wonder what a heart attack feels like. Can a man self-induce a heart attack from stress?

Perversely I wonder if my death by heart attack would solve the whole thing. I die. Rachael and the baby leave and go home. Popular opposition to Henry as chief disappears overnight, and the work is able to continue under Jeff's leadership. One half of my brain is spinning with these thoughts while the other half tells it to shut up and be cool.

I have always had a vivid imagination and the more rational part of my mind has always regarded that imagination as an unrelenting pain in the rear.

I haven't had coffee in two days. My head is splitting. My chest is constricting. I'm sweating. I can't breathe and I can hear the sound of my own pulse. I didn't even know that was possible. But before I can tumble further into mindlessness, there is more movement in the square.

The entire group of men takes two more steps backward, away from each other. If they were playing Simon Says, these would have been called "baby steps."

At the same time they cross both forearms in front of their stomachs, exposing their chins. To Americans this won't look like much. To the Kilo it is a near impossibility.

This is the universal Kilo signal of disarmament. Crossing your arms over your stomach and leaving your chin exposed is the Kilo equivalent of an American football player taking off his helmet and letting it hang by his side.

He hasn't given up and gone away, but he has openly taken himself out of the fight. It always happens in Kilo confrontations, but only by one side.

Never two.

The effect of every man doing so simultaneously is electric. Two minutes ago the air was thick with violence. "Tense" wouldn't have even begun to describe it.

What we have just witnessed is de-escalation on a mass scale. I am conscious of the fact that I am once again gaping – literally open mouthed – at the scene before me.

I can't stop staring.

The closest possible parallel I can conjure up in the moment is the famous Christmas Day truce during World War One. There was fighting and violence and killing; and then, by some unspoken agreement, there wasn't.

I can only hope that this particular truce isn't temporary, but I can't see any possible reason why it wouldn't be.

"Do you think that they –" I start to ask but Jeff silences me with a shake of his head.

I bite off the rest of my question and follow the direction of his eyes to the far side of the square. There, standing in the tree line, is Henry.

He is motionless and half hidden by foliage. His pose does not match that of the men. He is poised for fighting. In his hand he holds a club, larger than the billy clubs of the younger men but smaller than those of the older men.

My every sense is heightened and the hope I felt a moment ago is gone. A rustle of leaves sounds from the right. It would have been inaudible on any other day, but the silence of the square ensures that no one misses the noise.

What I see both surprises and horrifies me. Palal is standing in the tree line, having affected the same pose as Henry. He too, is poised and ready for a fight, his weapon somewhat larger but essentially the same as the one in Henry's own hand.

I have been unconsciously holding my breath; and I force myself to exhale, trying to be as silent as I can.

I manage one breath and then another.

I can feel my heart rate begin to slow as the oxygen floods my body.

I flinch as Palal steps forward, walking purposefully into the square but never removing his hand from his chin. Swiveling my head, I look across to see Henry doing the same. In direct contrast to the immobile men around them, their movements are confident and swift.

They stride toward one another with a calm inevitability that chills my blood even as a fresh layer of sweat breaks out on my forehead.

They are moving with a detachment that seems at once clinical and fatalistic, but it stops just as abruptly as it began. Henry and Palal face each other from a distance of less than four feet – striking distance.

I have never been a patient person and I am at my breaking point. The continual waiting and staring, the stopping and starting, the posing and posturing – it is all too much. I marvel at the composure of the men.

My work and my jungle mission career hang in the balance, but they each stand to lose far more. If things do not go their way, one side will lose not only their homes, but perhaps their families and their lives as well.

Henry and Palal are frozen in place. But then, like animated statues, they begin to move. As each man uncurls the fingers on his left hand he slowly lowers his hand to his side.

As their hands pass the invisible line of their waists they transfer their clubs, now holding them by the wrong end in their other hand. This is what submission looks like to a Kilo warrior.

To expose your chin in a signal of peace is one thing. But to grasp your weapon in the non-dominant hand indicates a posture of complete non-aggression.

"Did they just –"Jeff starts to ask. This time, I silence him.

At first nothing else happens.

The stare down continues. But as I look at the men facing each other across the rainy square, I do not pick up the same hostility as before. The emotions being broadcast aren't exactly friendly, but neither are they menacing.

Wary and suspicious is more accurate – more like a prosecutor and a defense attorney meeting to negotiate a plea bargain than boxers in pre-fight standoff. What happens over the next two minutes is something I'll never forget. It is such a cliché to say that, but with confusion clouding my mind and the rain and the tension and the absolute newness of it all, it is the best I can come up with right now.

Henry and Palal continue to look at each other with wary eyes.

The men arrayed behind them silently close ranks until they are shoulder to shoulder and standing in a straight line.

The earlier parentheses arrangement is gone, replaced by a tight grouping of men. Two men from the far end of Henry's side step forward, turn, and align themselves on the far side of Palal's end. One man from Palal's side steps forward, turns, and joins Henry's group.

Each side fans back out, assuming their previous positions.

Henry and Palal never look away, but they do exchange a short burst of words. The conversation is low and inaudible to us, but it has an immediate effect. Palal gives out a call not unlike a monkey call – low and shrill at the same time. It is the Kilo call to form up for a journey.

Normally only employed by the chief, it is disconcerting to hear it coming from Palal. Does this mean he is the chief now? Where are they all going? Village-wide excursions normally only occur when the village is under threat of imminent attack.

There is movement from the open sided pavilion. Women and children come out from under the roof. Teenagers step aside and children are scooped up. Roughly half the people gathered there begin to cross the square. They are carrying bundles. I couldn't see the bundles earlier. They must have set them on the floor, out of sight behind the walls.

Each woman carries a bundle low on her back, attached by a wide strap around the shoulders. Small children totter along with older ones bringing up the rear.

They move soundlessly across the wet ground, circling around to the back of Palal's men. They are a solemn group, showing no emotion.

All at once it hits me: the end of the violence, the men changing sides, the whistle, and the women packed to go. There is going to be a journey; but not everyone is going, only the people on Palal's side.

No, I silently correct myself, only the people *not* on Henry's side.

There is a difference.

A Kilo does not have to be in love with the idea of a certain man as his chief in order to follow him. He simply has to recognize it as the least worst option.

This will be a journey, but it's a one way trip.

The group slowly backs away, keeping their eyes to the front. Only Palal remains with the others. A bird call sounds out, and Palal and Henry lower their weapons.

Palal follows his men into the tree line.

The rain has slowed, and for a moment all is still. The Kilo who disappeared into the tree line have melted away completely. Other than the footprints they left in the rain softened ground, there remains no visible trace. The jungle has absorbed them without effort. They have simply vanished.

12

Later that night I am sitting around the fire pit with my wife and my friends. Jeff and I had left the square as quietly as we could, somehow sensing that we should not be part of whatever came next for the people who were left.

A few hours later we were visited by Henry who filled us in. There are ancient ways, he said, of ensuring the survival of a tribe. They do not happen often because they involve significant loss of pride, and all too often men would rather die fighting than face public shame.

After the tree had fallen and scattered the fight the day before, Henry and Palal met in the jungle in secret.

Although they disagreed over specifics, in essence they both saw the tree's destruction the same way Rachael had. It was the work of supernatural forces, and it scared them into peace talks where they were able to reach an agreement.

Palal and any who wished would be allowed to leave peacefully, taking their possessions with them. Henry also agreed to allow the families of the men to leave with them, along with extra food and supplies enough to start a new village.

Nothing about the fight itself was discussed, but I wonder if it didn't come down to pragmatism and survival instinct. Palal had most of the elders and experienced men on his side, but they *were* older.

If the confrontation had continued, the younger men would have won.

What they lacked in hunting experience and village prestige, they more than made up for in speed and strength. I have dozens of questions that will have to keep for another day.

We are thrilled, but our hearts are hurting. Almost half the village followed Palal. They will establish their own settlement far off into the jungle – "a journey of one moon or more," according to Henry.

They will be far enough away that rival hunters will not have to risk a chance encounter, but close enough to remain part of collective Kilo memory. They are neither enemies nor friends, just people who used to know each other.

Henry is the undisputed chief. The airstrip will be his privilege garden after all. Whether that is helpful or harmful remains to be seen. The people who remain are not necessarily of one mind. Their reasons for staying are diverse.

Some are his relatives and would have followed if he had left. Others are beginning to see the truth of Kaale and want to hear more. Some are indifferent and I am sure there a few who are just happy to be rid of Palal.

Rachael never let go of that baby.

She won't give it up to be killed, but she didn't want to lose her house.

Henry made it clear that enough of the remaining people believe evil spirits follow the child, and they remain uneasy because of that belief.

The compromise we settled on was that the baby could live, so long as she lived with us – outside the village in our jungle suburb.

Until it becomes apparent that the evil spirits have left her alone and have pursued other targets, she is not welcome in a Kilo dwelling, or in the village proper.

As a show of good faith and a nod of cooperation, we have agreed to allow a Kilo shaman to "cleanse and protect" our home from the spirits.

We are sitting in the back yard while he does his thing in the house. The smells wafting from the open windows are at once intoxicating and repulsive.

I have no idea what he's doing, and I'm not about to go in and find out. All I know is that when he's done the house will be considered clean.

Of course we know this is all ridiculous; but we felt it had to be done. Jeff and I are still not sure we have made the right decision on this one.

Did we set back the work by saving the baby? I hate to think so, but it is a possibility.

Have we compromised spiritually by letting the shaman into our home to perform his rituals? I don't know.

Have we discredited our witness or harmed the reputation of Christ by cooperating with false religion? I hope not.

No doubt people back home will find fault with what we did, but they weren't here and they can never truly understand.

In the end, it was one of those calls that only a missionary on the ground can make.

Headquarters can't help you with it; you're on your own. We did the best we could with what we had. We're just praying that it is good enough.

Our work of learning the Kilo language will continue slow and steady as it did before – a tortoise, not a hare. The goal is still the same: to produce a Bible written in the Kilo language and plant a self-sustaining Kilo church to outlive us all.

These recent events may have pushed our time table back, but that's okay. We came here thinking that we would never be parents.

If we had been thinking, we wouldn't have thought that.

I look over at Rachael and the baby in her arms, and I am immediately crying. She isn't "the baby" anymore. Her mother and family left with Palal. She is our daughter now. Her name is Dinah. It means *"judged"* or *"vindicated"* and she is the newest member of our team – a native born jungle missionary!

Death is no Stranger

Acknowledgements

Writing a book is largely an exercise in solitude. Bringing it to print is not. Sincere thanks go to each of the following people for their essential contributions in the making of this book:

To my wife **Natalie,** for perceiving before anyone else that a novel about Tribal Missions could be a reality and for giving me the encouragement to make it so.

To **Marianne Thurmond,** for editing the book. Editors make the world safe for reading and you are one of the best!

To **Noah Bowman,** for creating the Kilo language using only the brain things inside of his head.

To **Carolyn White**, for being my first reader and on-call English expert.

To the missionaries and staff at every level of **Ethnos360**. You formed much of my motivation and inspiration for writing and you are gospel heroes. Every dollar of proceeds from the Jungle Missionary Series is sent right back into the work. Learn more at: www.ethnos360.org

To you, **the reader**. Thank you for reading and getting to know Ian. Now "go thou and do likewise," until the whole world hears!

I love to hear from readers and I promise to respond back if you want to contact me. You can reach me at: **erniebowmanauthor@gmail.com**

About the Author

Ernie Bowman is the Associate Pastor of Calvary Baptist Church in Ypsilanti, Michigan. He is a graduate of Faith Baptist Bible College (Ankeny, Iowa) and Maranatha Baptist Seminary (Watertown, Wisconsin).

He also teaches high school Bible and coaches soccer at Washtenaw Christian Academy in Saline, Michigan. Ernie writes a weekly blog about Christian living, reading, and sports. You can find his work online at **www.thefoolish1.com**.

Ernie Bowman

Don't Miss:

See how it all started in Book 1 of the Jungle Missionary Series!

An exciting discovery has the tribe convinced that a mythical creature has returned and must be hunted down to protect the village. When the hunt takes a dark turn, the missionaries are faced with life-and-death choices they never thought they would have to make.

The stakes are high in *Legend of the Wapa!*

Available from Cruciform Press

www.cruciformpress.com
www.amazon.com

Also available from Ernie Bowman:

A Surgeon's Hands – God's Work will transport you into the exotic world of medical missions and tropical surgery. For four decades, Dr. Bob Cropsey was a missionary surgeon in Togo, Africa. His goal was to use medical care to establish a gospel witness, and he accomplished that with undeniable success. *A Surgeon's Hands – God's Work* tells the story of a man used by God to help found two hospitals, plant numerous churches, raise a family, and save lives on the frontier of modern missions.

Not only will you gape at Dr. Bob's adventures, but you will also be challenged to emulate his courage and conviction. This stunning account of tropical surgery and missions miracles portrays the fast-moving life story of Bob and Shirley Cropsey, leaving you astonished at the great God they serve and the remarkable work he has done through them. This is not a book to be missed!

*Available now at **Amazon.com***

Made in the USA
Monee, IL
24 July 2021